T0153513

THE CLOCKWORK MAN

THE CLOCKWORK MAN

by

E.V. ODLE

introduction by **ANNALEE NEWITZ**

—

HiLoBooks
powered by **Cursor**
Boston, MA *and* **Brooklyn, NY**
2013

HiLoBooks
RADIUM AGE SCIENCE FICTION

The Scarlet Plague
Jack London
Comment by Matthew Battles

With the Night Mail *and* "As Easy as A.B.C."
Rudyard Kipling
Comments by Matthew De Abaitua & Bruce Sterling

The Poison Belt
Arthur Conan Doyle
Comments by Joshua Glenn & Gordon Dahlquist

When the World Shook
H. Rider Haggard
Comments by James Parker & J.R. Bickley, M.R.C.S.

People of the Ruins
Edward Shanks
Comment by Tom Hodgkinson

The Night Land
William Hope Hodgson
Comment by Erik Davis

Goslings
J.D. Beresford
Comment by Astra Taylor

The Clockwork Man
E.V. Odle
Comment by Annalee Newitz

Theodore Savage
Cicely Hamilton
Comment by Gary Panter

The Man with Six Senses
Muriel Jaeger
Comment by Mark Kingwell

Series Foreword © Joshua Glenn 2012–13
Introduction © Annalee Newitz 2013

This edition of *The Clockwork Man* follows the text
of the 1923 edition published by Doubleday, Page &
Company, which is in the public domain.

Library of Congress Control Number: 2013932621
ISBN: 978-1-935869-63-4

Cover illustration © Michael Lewy 2013
Cover design by Tony Leone, Leone Design
Page and text design by Colleen Venable

PRINTED IN THE UNITED STATES OF AMERICA

The mission of HiLoBooks is to serialize and
otherwise popularize forgotten Radium Age
science fiction via the website HiLobrow.com, and
to reissue some of these texts as paperback books.
Both HiLobrow.com and HiLoBooks are edited
by Joshua Glenn, and published by KING MIXER.

For more information, visit HiLobrow.com/HiLoBooks
Follow us on Twitter: @hilobrow

HiLoBooks is grateful to Richard Nash for his vision
and publishing acumen.

POWERED BY CURSOR

DISTRIBUTED BY PUBLISHERS GROUP WEST
10 9 8 7 6 5 4 3 2 1

TABLE *of* CONTENTS

RADIUM AGE SCIENCE FICTION
Series Foreword by **Joshua Glenn**

SEVERAL YEARS AGO, I read Brian Aldiss's *Billion Year Spree*—his "true history of science fiction" from Mary Shelley to the early 1970s. I admire Aldiss tremendously, and I found his account of the genre's development entertaining and informative... but something bothered me, after I'd finished reading the book. Something was missing.

Billion Year Spree is terrific on the topic of science fiction from *Frankenstein* through the "scientific romances" of Verne, Poe, and Wells—and also terrific on science fiction's so-called Golden Age, the start of which sf exegetes date to John W. Campbell's 1937 assumption of the editorship of the magazine *Astounding*. However, regarding science fiction published between the beginning of the Golden Age and the end of the Verne-Poe-Wells "scientific romance" era, Aldiss (who rightly laments that Wells's 20th century fiction after, perhaps, 1904's *The Food of the Gods*, fails to recapture "that darkly beautiful quality of imagination, or that instinctive-seeming unity of construction, which lives in his early novels") has very little to say.

Aldiss seems to feel that authors of science fiction after Wells but before the Golden Age weren't very talented. He certainly doesn't think much of the literary skills of Hugo Gernsback, sometimes called the "Father of Science Fiction," who founded *Amazing Stories* in 1926 and coined the phrase "science fiction" while he was at it. He's right: Gernsback's story-telling abilities were as primitive as his ideas were advanced. But does that justify skipping over the 1904-33 era? (By my reckoning, Campbell and his cohort first began to develop their literate, analytical, socially conscious science fiction in reaction to the 1934 advent of the campy *Flash Gordon* comic strip, not to mention Hollywood's "sci-fi" blockbusters that sought to ape the success of 1933's *King Kong*. In other words, sf's Golden Age began before 1937; if I had to pick a year, I'd say 1934.) Is Aldiss's animus against that era due solely to style and quality? I suspect not.

Aldiss's book is hardly alone in sweeping pre-1934 science fiction under the rug. During the so-called Golden Age, which was given that moniker not after the fact, but *at the time*, as a way of signifying the end of science fiction's post-Wells Dark Age, Campbellians took pains to distinguish their own science fiction from everything that had been published in the genre (with the sole exception of 1932's *Brave New World*) since 1904. In his influential 1958 critique, *New Maps of Hell*, for example, Kingsley Amis noted that mature science fiction first established itself in the mid-1930s, "separating with a slowly increasing decisiveness from [immature] fantasy and space-opera." And in his introduction to a 1974 collection, *Before the Golden Age*, editor Isaac Asimov apologetically notes that although it certainly possessed an exuberant vigor, the pre-Golden Age science fiction he grew up reading "seems, to anyone who has experienced the Campbell Revolution, to be clumsy, primitive, naive."

We should be suspicious of this Cold War-era rhetoric of maturity! I'm reminded of Reinhold Niebuhr's pronunciamento, at a 1952 *Partisan Review* symposium, that the utopianism of the early 20th century ought to be regarded as "an adolescent embarrassment." Perhaps Golden Age science fiction's stars—Asimov, Robert Heinlein, Ray Bradbury, and so forth—were regarded as an improvement on their predecessors because in their stories utopian visions and schemes were treated with cynicism. Liberal and conservative anti-utopians who point out that pre-Cold War utopian narratives often demonstrate a naive and perhaps proto-totalitarian eagerness to force square pegs into round holes via thought control and coercion are not wrong. I wouldn't want to live in one of those utopias. However, I strongly agree with those who argue that the intellectual abandonment of utopianism since the 1930s has sapped our political options, and left us all in the helpless position of passive accomplices.

Sure, some 1904-33 science fiction—Gernsback, Edgar Rice Burroughs, and E.E. "Doc" Smith, for example—is indeed fantastical and primitive (though it's still fun to read today). But many other authors of that period—including Olaf Stapledon, William Hope Hodgson, Karel Čapek, Charlotte Perkins Gilman, and Yevgeny Zamyatin—gave us science fiction that was literate, analytical, socially conscious… and also utopian. Utopian in the sense that whatever their politics, Radium Age authors found in the newly named "science fiction" genre a fitting vehicle to express their faith, or at least their hope, that another world is possible. That worldview may have seemed embarrassingly adolescent from the late 1930s until, say, the fall of the Berlin Wall. But today it's an inspiring vision.

—*Joshua Glenn*
  Cofounder, HiLobrow.com & HiLoBooks
  Boston, 2012

THE FIRST CYBORG AND THE FIRST SINGULARITY
Introduction by **Annalee Newitz**

IF YOU DON'T stop making war on each other, one day women will team up with benevolent, naked aliens and implant you with a clock that controls your behavior and sends you into a timeless multiverse. Oh and also? That timeless multiverse will be full of hat and wig stores.

This is the warning expressed in E.V. Odle's 1923 novel *The Clockwork Man,* and the goofiness is intentional. One of Odle's preoccupations in this story is the way truly futuristic ideas strike us as hilarious. As his witty but conservative character Allingham observes, humanity's most pernicious defense against change is an ability to turn anything into a joke. When our characters first observe the Clockwork man, a peculiar cyborg from thousands of years in the future, he's gone glitchy. He's spouting odd phrases and stumbling awkwardly through a small town cricket match. Their first impulse is to laugh at him, and this is perhaps more chilling than their subsequent excitement and terror as they realize what he really is.

The Clockwork Man is one of the first cyborg novels ever written, and undoubtedly Odle was anticipating his audience's snorts of derision at his bizarre creation: a human man whose skull is implanted with an elaborate clock mechanism which he comically covers with a hat and wig. But he was not the only writer obsessed with synthetic humans in 1923. Karel Čapek's classic robot uprising play *R.U.R.* came out that year as well. The play introduced the word "robot" and stole the spotlight from Odle's weirder tale.

Unlike the synthetic workers of *R.U.R.,* the Clockwork man was born a human. But his nervous system, brain, and body have been enhanced with technology: he does not die, he is exceptionally strong, he can sense physical phenomena beyond the capacity of the human mind, and his physical attributes can be changed with the poke of a knob. Ordinarily, he explains, he exists in a multiverse where all his desires are satisfied simply through a kind of "conjuring" of whatever he wants. He's especially stumped by the way humans are always putting finite objects into finite places. In the Clockwork man's distant future, all objects can be anywhere, anytime.

The Clockwork man, in other words, has returned from beyond what today's science fiction writers would call the Singularity—and he finds our limited world bewildering, though ultimately seductive.

It's striking how many obsessions of contemporary science fiction show up in Odle's novel. Using this mechanized man, Odle is able to muse on might happen to humanity after what Singulatarians call "the intelligence explosion" when the human mind is enhanced beyond all recognition by merging with computers. The Clockwork man seems to come from a virtual world of infinite plenitude, much the way uploaded people do in the work of Iain M. Banks and Ken MacLeod.

Embedded in the figure of the cyborg, from his very first appearance in literature, is the idea of a Singularity which involves virtual worlds and brain implants. There's even a kind of dawning knowledge of the "uncanny valley," a late twentieth century theory that describes the feeling of revulsion and hilarity inspired by robots who look almost human, but not quite. Something about the para-humanity of the Clockwork man's appearance makes people burst into laughter, or throw up—or bite their lips to prevent both.

As the novel unfolds, we learn that the Clockwork man has fallen back into linear time, thousands of years in his past, because his mechanism is broken. He's stuck in 1923, in our monoverse, and he bears a garbled message from the future to three men whose lives he changes forever. These men, the middle-aged doctor Allingham, the recent Cambridge grad Gregg, and the young dreamer Arthur, respond very differently to the prospect of humanity's mechanized future. And those responses hinge in part on their view of women.

Odle was writing at a time when women's rights were an enormously important issue of the day, and female political power loomed as a futuristic threat and promise. Odle lived for many years in the Bloomsbury district of London with his wife Rose, and these issues would have been fused with the dominant literary figures of his generation. Not only was he living in the same neighborhood as writers like Virginia Woolf, but Odle's older brother was married to the bohemian author Dorothy Richardson. She is often credited with writing the first stream-of-consciousness novel in English (*Pointed Roofs*), and she dated H.G. Wells for many years before settling down with Alan Odle. In Rose Odle's autobiography, *Salt of Our Youth*, she recalls that Richardson's mentor J.D. Beresford, author of the SF novels *The Hampdenshire Wonder* and *Goslings*, helped Odle publish his first novel, *The History of Alfred Rudd*, the year before *The Clockwork Man* came out. Through his family associations, Odle would have been exposed to a world where women dominated the artistic scene.

It's no surprise, then, that the stuffy doctor Allingham's horror at the Clockwork man is paralleled only by his horror at the radical ideas about woman's equality espoused by his fiancée Lillian. Cyborgs and women represent the future, and not just metaphorically. In a fascinating passage toward the end of the novel, Odle explores how Allingham's conflicts with Lillian, if left unresolved, could result in a gender apocalypse.

As the novel reaches its climax, Lillian is considering calling the marriage off because she believes Allingham wants her to be a traditional wife who spends all her time doing housework and managing his affairs. She's also dismayed by his habit of turning everything into a joke—an issue that ties into Odle's larger point about humor as a defense against the future. Allingham reluctantly admits that she has a legitimate point of view, but their conflict is never quite resolved.

While Allingham and Lillian discuss their relationship, the Clockwork man figures out how to fix his broken mechanism. But he remains in our timeline long enough to have a strange conversation with young Arthur. Arthur has been struggling to make enough money to marry his beloved Rose (no doubt named for Odle's wife, to whom he also dedicated the novel), who doesn't care a fig for conventions that say men should be breadwinners. She's encouraging him to pursue his dream, which is to become a writer. Unlike Allingham, who can barely see his way forward into a future where women are his equals, Arthur is already inhabiting that future. He's contemplating shedding the conventional male breadwinner role, and his future wife is encouraging it.

When the Clockwork man wanders down a country road and sees Arthur and Rose embracing, he decides to tell Arthur why the future is full of men like himself. The young couple's love has reminded him that his incredible superpowers come at the expense of emotions. With tears running down his face, he explains that the clockwork men are the creation of "makers," creatures who arrived upon the scene "after the last wars." It's unclear whether these makers are aliens or advanced humans, but we know they don't wear clothes and are "very clever, and very mild and gentle." The Clockwork man also describes them as "real," unlike himself.

He tells the open-mouthed Arthur that men of the future became so obsessed with war that the makers allied with women—also "real"—and banished men from their world. Men's destructiveness, and their inability to perceive the realness of women, were their downfall. This is Allingham and Lillian's conflict over gender roles writ large. The cyborg explains that men left the makers no choice but to "shut us up in the clocks," and give them "the world we wanted," absent of emotion but filled with infinite power and resources.

Here it becomes clear that the Clockwork man lives mostly in a virtual world, "the clock," rather than the "real" world that is apparently still inhabited by women and makers. He's an analog version of an upload, and his world of plenitude is also a prison. In this scenario we see echoes of early feminist SF like Charlotte Perkins Gilman's 1915 *Herland*, as well as the anxieties expressed by pundits like Henry Adams, who noted in his 1905 book *The Education of Henry Adams* that women would achieve equality in part by "marrying machinery."

While it's temping to say that *The Clockwork Man*'s narrative arc is informed primarily by feminism, as Odle's frequent references to Einsteinian physics and evolutionary theory attest, it is also strongly influenced by the ways science was transforming our understanding of the world. Plus, it was written under the shadow of World War I. Odle worked as the foreman at a munitions factory during the war; his vision of a battle-mangled future was surely spawned by his experience.

Perhaps most importantly, however, this novel is the product of a time and place where pulp fiction and literature overlapped. In 1926, three years after publishing *The Clockwork Man*, Odle became the first editor of popular British literary magazine *The Argosy* (not to be confused with the American pulp magazine of the same name), which specialized in reprinting short stories by luminaries like Wells, Joseph Conrad, and Oscar Wilde.

When Odle began his fourteen-year tenure as editor of *The Argosy*, the magazine was devoted to literature but it was published in pulp-sized format. So it would have looked like *Weird Tales*—or the American *Argosy*—but it featured short stories by literary authors. As pulp magazine historian Mike Ashley told me, it was also one of Britain's best-selling magazines, despite being reprint. Odle's great genius was an uncanny ability to bring little-known stories to public attention: According to Ashley, Odle and his editorial team scoured *Argosy* parent company Cassell's magazine archive and other sources "to find unusual and rewarding stories, usually by well-known writers, but where the story itself was little known." The magazine Odle created was so successful that it continued into the 1970s, several decades after his early death in 1942.

To understand the narrative construction of *The Clockwork Man*, we must view it as a book on the boundary between pulp and literature. Its ending isn't merely an "as you know, Bob" infodump; it's also part of an ambiguous web of possibilities stemming from the characters' variations in perspective.

While Allingham views the Clockwork man's future as frighteningly unimaginable, Gregg realizes that it's actually not very different from the contemporary world. When the two men come across the cyborg's lost hat, they find a tag inside from Dunn & Co., a popular London men's clothing manufacturer in 1923—which, in the Clockwork man's future, has been a going concern for 2,000 years (the real-life Dunn & Co. closed its doors in the 1970s). Gregg realizes that immortal life inside the clock has allowed men to perpetuate ancient institutions long after they would have naturally perished in the real world. There's an inherent conservatism in the Singularity, which allows men to transcend time only to foreclose the possibility of future changes.

Then there is the novel's key revelation, which is that the Clockwork man is just one possible future for humanity. We won't all be imprisoned/liberated by the clock. Many humans exist in the real world of makers and women. Like a pulp fiction writer, Odle gives us a grotesque future jammed with aliens, robots and Einsteinian wonders; but like a literary Modernist, he refuses to define that as the only pathway to tomorrow. There are many futures, many perspectives, and many possibilities. Allingham and Lillian's relationship hints at the conflict that forces women to banish men to the clock. Arthur and Rose's romance figures a "gentle" future of makers and women living together in naked harmony. And the Clockwork man's hat gooses us into remembering that even a shockingly futuristic vision may be, at its core, a fundamentally reactionary enterprise.

Thanks to Jess Nevins for research aid!

"Consciousness in a mere automaton is a useless and unnecessary epiphenomenon."
— Prof. Lloyd Morgan

CHAPTER 1

The Coming of the Clockwork Man

I

IT WAS JUST as Doctor Allingham had congratulated himself upon the fact that the bowling was broken, and he had only to hit now and save the trouble of running, just as he was scanning the boundaries with one eye and with the other following Tanner's short, crooked arm raised high above the white sheet at the back of the opposite wicket, that he noticed the strange figure. Its abrupt appearance, at first sight like a scarecrow dumped suddenly on the horizon, caused him to lessen his grip upon the bat in his hand. His mind wandered for just that fatal moment, and his vision of the oncoming bowler was swept away and its place taken by that arresting figure of a man coming over the path at the top of the hill, a man whose attitude, on closer examination, seemed extraordinarily like another man in the act of bowling.

That was why its effect was so distracting. It seemed to the doctor that the figure had popped up there on purpose to imitate the action of a bowler and so baulk him. During the fraction of a second in which the ball reached him, this second image had blotted out everything else. But the behavior of the figure was certainly abnormal. Its movements were violently ataxic. Its arms revolved like sails of a windmill. Its legs shot out in all directions, enveloped in dust.

The doctor's astonishment was turned into annoyance by the spectacle of his shattered wicket. A vague clatter of applause broke out. The wicket keeper stooped down to pick up the bails. The fielders relaxed and flopped down on the grass. They seemed to have discovered suddenly that it was a hot afternoon, and that cricket was, after all, a comparatively strenuous game. One of the umpires, a sly nasty fellow, screwed up his eyes and looked hard at the doctor as the latter passed him, walking with the slow, meditative gait of the bowled out, and swinging his gloves. There was nothing to do but glare back, and make the umpire feel a worm. The doctor wore an eye-glass, and he succeeded admirably. His irritation boiled over and produced a sense of ungovernable childish rage. Somehow, he had not been able to make any runs this season, and his bowling average was all to pieces. He began to think he ought to give up cricket. He was getting past the age when a man can accept reverses in the spirit of the game, and he was sick and tired of seeing his name every week in the *Great Wymering Gazette* as having been dismissed for a "mere handful."

He despised himself for feeling such intense annoyance. It was extraordinary how, as one grew older, it became less possible to restrain primitive and savage impulses. When things went wrong, you wanted to do something violent and unforgivable, something you would regret afterwards, but which you would be quite willing to do for the sake of immediate satisfaction. As he approached the pavilion, he wanted to charge into the little group of players gathered around the scoring table—he wanted to rush at them and clump their heads with his bat. His mind was so full of ridiculous impulse that his body actually bolted forward as though to carry it out, and he stumbled slightly. It was absurd to feel like this, every little incident pricking him to the point of exasperation, everything magnified and translated into a conspiracy against him. Someone was manipulating the metal figure plates on the back index board. He saw a "1" hung up for the last player. Surely he had made more than One! All that swiping and thwacking, all that anxiety and suspense, and nothing to show for it! But, he remembered, he had only scored once, and that had been a lucky scramble. The fielders had been tantalisingly alert. They had always been just exactly where he had thought they were not.

He passed into the interior of the pavilion. Someone said, "Hard luck, Allingham," and he kept his eyes to the ground for fear that malice might shoot from them. He flung his bat in a corner and sat down to unstrap his pads. Gregg, the captain, came in. He was a cool, fair young man, fresh from Cambridge. He came in grinning, and only stopped when he saw the expression on Allingham's face.

"I thought you were pretty well set," he remarked casually.

"So I was," said Allingham, aiming a pad at the opposite wall. "So I was. I never felt more like it in my life. Then some idiot goes and sticks himself right over the top of the sheet. An escaped lunatic, a chap with a lot of extra arms and legs. You never saw anything like it in your life!"

"Really," said Gregg, and grinned again. "H'm," he remarked presently, "six wickets down, and all the best men out. We look like going to pieces. Especially as we're a man short."

"Well, I can't help it," said Allingham, "you don't expect a thing like that to happen. What's the white sheet for? So you can see the bowler's arm. But when something gets in the way, just over the sheet—just where you've got your eyes fixed. It wouldn't happen once in a million times."

"Never mind," said Gregg, cheerfully, "it's all in the game."

"It *isn't* in the game," Allingham began. But the other had gone out.

Allingham stood up and slowly rolled down his sleeves and put on his blazer. Of course, Gregg was like that, a thorough sportsman, taking the good with the bad. But then he was only twenty-four. You could be like that then, so full of life and high spirits that generosity flowed from you imperceptibly and without effort. At forty you began to shrivel up. Atrophy of the finer feelings. You began to be deliberately and consistently mean and narrow. You took a savage delight in making other people pay for your disappointments.

He looked out of the window, and there was that confounded figure still jiggling about. It had come nearer to the ground. It hovered, with a curious air of not being related to its surroundings that was more than puzzling. It did not seem to know what it was about, but hopped along aimlessly, as though scenting a track, stopped for a moment, blundered forward again and made a zig-zag course towards the ground. The doctor watched it advancing through the broad meadow that bounded the pitch, threading its way between the little groups of grazing cows, that raised their heads with more than their ordinary, slow persistency, as though startled by some noise. The figure seemed to be aiming for the barrier of hurdles that surrounded the pitch, but whether its desire was for cricket or merely to reach some kind of goal, whether it sought recreation or a mere pause from its restless convulsions, it was difficult to tell. Finally, it fell against the fence and hung there, two hands crooked over the hurdle and its legs drawn together at the knees. It became suddenly very still—so still that it was hard to believe it had ever moved.

It was certainly odd. The doctor was so struck by something altogether *wrong* about the figure, something so suggestive of a pathological phenomenon, that he almost forgot his annoyance and remained watching it with an unlighted cigarette between his lips.

II

There was another person present at the cricket match to whom the appearance of the strange figure upon the hill seemed an unusual circumstance, only in his case it provided rather an agreeable diversion than an irritating disturbance. It had been something to look at, and much more interesting than cricket. All afternoon Arthur Withers had been lying in the long grass, chewing bits of it at intervals and hoping against hope that something would happen to prevent his having to go out to the pitch and make a fool of himself. He knew perfectly well that Tanner, the demon bowler of the opposing team, would get him out first ball. He might linger at the seat of operations whilst one or two byes were run; but there were few quests more unwarranted and hopeless than that excursion, duly padded and gloved, to the scene of instant disaster. He dreaded the unnecessary trouble he was bound to give, the waiting while he walked with shaking knees to the wicket; the careful assistance of the umpire in finding centre for him; all the ceremony of cricket rehearsed for his special and quite undeserved benefit. And afterwards he would be put to field where there was a lot of running to do, and only dead balls to pick up. Of course he wasn't funking; that wouldn't be cricket. But he had been very miserable. He sometimes wondered why he paid a subscription to take part in the game that cost him such agony of mind to play. But it was the privilege that mattered as much as anything. Just to be allowed to play.

Arthur was accustomed to be allowed to do things. He accepted his fate with a broad grin and determination to do whatever was cricket in life.

Everybody in Great Wymering knew that he was a bit of a fool, and rather simple. They knew that his career at the bank had been one wild story of mistakes and narrow escapes from dismissal. But even that didn't really matter. Things happened to him just as much as to other and more efficient individuals, little odd circumstances that made the rest of life curiously unimportant by comparison. Every day, for example, something humorous occurred in life, something that obliterated all the worries, something worth waking up in the middle of the night to laugh at it again. That is why the appearance of the odd-looking figure had been so welcome to him. It was distinctly amusing. It had made him forget his fears. Like all funny things or happenings, it made you for the moment impersonal.

He was so interested that presently he got up and wandered along the line of hurdles towards the spot where the strange figure had come to rest. It had not moved at all, and this fact added astonishment to curiosity. It clung desperately to the barrier, as though glad to have got there. Its attitude was awkward in the extreme, hunched up, ill-adjusted, but it made no attempt to achieve comfort. Further along, little groups of spectators were leaning against the barrier in nearly similar positions, smoking pipes, fidgeting and watching the game intently. But the strange figure was not doing anything at all, and if he looked at the players it was with an unnatural degree of intense observation. Arthur walked slowly along, wondering how close he could get to his objective without appearing rude. But, somehow, he did not think this difficulty would arise. There was something singularly forlorn and wretched about this curious individual, a suggestion of inconsequence. Arthur could have sworn that he was homeless and had no purpose or occupation. He was not in the picture of life, but something blobbed on by accident. Other people gave some sharp hint by their manner or deportment that they belonged to some roughly defined class. You could guess something about them. But this extraordinary personage, who had emerged so suddenly from the line of the sky and streaked aimlessly across the landscape, bore not even the vaguest marks of homely origin. He had staggered along the path, not with the recognisable gait of a drunken man, but with a sort of desperate decision, as though convinced in his mind that the path he was treading was really only a thin plank stretched from heaven to earth upon which he had been obliged to balance himself. And now he was hanging upon the hurdle, and it was just as though someone had thrown a great piece of clay there, and with a few deft strokes shaped it into the vague likeness of a man.

III

As he drew nearer, Arthur's impression of an unearthly being was sobered a little by the discovery that the strange figure wore a wig. It was a very red wig, and over the top of it was jammed a brown bowler hat. The face underneath was crimson and flabby. Arthur decided that it was not a very interesting face. Its features seemed to melt into each other in an odd sort of way, so that you knew that you were looking at a face and that was about all. He was about to turn his head politely and pass on, when he was suddenly rooted to the ground by the observation of a most singular circumstance.

The strange figure was flapping his ears—flapping them violently backwards and forwards with an almost inconceivable rapidity!

Arthur felt a sudden clutching sensation in the region of his heart. Of course, he had heard of people being able to move their ears slightly. That was common knowledge. But the ears of this man positively vibrated. They were more like the wings of some strange insect than human ears. It was a ghastly spectacle—unbelievable, yet obvious. Arthur tried to walk away; he looked this way and that, but it was impossible to resist the fascination of those flapping ears. Besides, the strange figure had seen him. He was fixing him with eyes that did not move in their sockets, but stared straight ahead; Arthur had placed himself in the direct line of their vision. The expression in the eyes was compelling, almost hypnotic.

"Excuse me," Arthur ventured, huskily, "did you wish to speak to me?"

The strange figure stopped flapping his ears and opened his mouth. He opened it unpleasantly wide, as though trying to yawn. Then he shut it with a sharp snap, and without yawning. After that he shifted his whole body very slowly, as though endeavoring to arouse himself from an enormous apathy.

And then he appeared to be waiting for something to happen.

Arthur fidgeted, and he looked nervously around him. It was an awkward situation, but after all, he had brought it on himself. He did not like to move away. Besides, having started the conversation it was only common politeness to wait until the stranger offered a remark. And presently, the latter opened his mouth again. This time he actually spoke.

"Wallabaloo—Wallabaloo—Bompadi—Bompadi—Wum. Wum—Wum—nine and ninepence—" he announced.

"I beg your pardon," said Arthur hastily.

"Wallabaloo," replied the other, eagerly. "Walla—Oh, hang it—Hulloa, now we've got it—Wallabaloo—No, we haven't—Bang Wallop—nine and ninepence—"

Arthur swallowed several times in rapid succession. His mind relapsed into a curious state of blankness. For some minutes he was not aware of any thinking processes at all. He began to feel dizzy and faint, from sheer bewilderment. And then the idea of escape crept into his consciousness. He moved one foot, intending to walk away. But the strange figure suddenly lifted up a hand, with an abrupt, jerky movement, like a signal jumping up. He said "nine and ninepence" three times very slowly and solemnly, and flapped his right ear twice. In spite of his confusion, Arthur could not help but noticing the peculiar and awful synchronisation of these movements. At any rate, they seemed to help this unfortunate individual out of his difficulties. Still holding a hand upright, he achieved his first complete sentence.

"*Not* an escaped lunatic," he protested, and tried to shake his head. But the attempt to do so merely started his ears flapping again.

And then, as though exhausted by these efforts, he relapsed altogether into a sort of lumpiness and general resemblance to nothing on earth. The hand dropped heavily. The ears twitched spasmodically, the right one reversing the action of the left. He seemed to sink down, like a deflated balloon, and a faint whistling sigh escaped his lips. His face assumed an expression that was humble in the extreme, as though he were desirous of apologising to the air for the bother of keeping him alive.

Arthur stared, expecting every moment to see the figure before him fall to the ground or even disappear through the earth. But just when his looseness and limpness reached to the lowest ebb a sudden pulse would shake the stranger from head to foot; noises that were scarcely human issued from him, puffings and blowings, a sort of jerky grinding and grating. He would rear up for a moment, appear alert and lively, only to collapse again, slowly and sadly, his head falling to one side, his arms fluttering feebly like the wings of a wounded bird.

Arthur's chief sensation was one of pity for a fellow creature obviously in such hopeless state. He almost forgot his alarm in his sympathy for the difficulties of the strange figure. That struggle to get alive, to produce the elementary effects of existence, made him think of his own moods of failure, his own helplessness. He took a step nearer to the hurdle.

"Can I *do* anything for you?" he enquired, almost in a whisper. Suddenly, the strange figure seemed to achieve a sort of mastery of himself. He began opening and shutting his mouth very rapidly, to the accompaniment of sharp clicking noises.

"It's devilish hard," he announced, presently, "this feeling, you know— Click—All dressed up and nowhere to go—Click—Click—"

"Is that how you feel? Arthur enquired. He came nearer still, as though to hear better. But the other got into a muddle with his affirmative. He flapped an ear in staccato fashion, and Arthur hastily withdrew.

Now, the afternoon was very warm and very still. Where they stood the only sounds that could reach them were the slight crack of the batted ball, and the soft padding of the fielders. That was why the thing that happened next could hardly be mistaken. It began by the strange figure suddenly putting both hands upon the hurdle and raising himself up about an inch off the ground. He looked all at once enormously alive and vital. Light flashed in his eyes.

"Eureka!" he clicked, "I'm working!"

"What's that?" shouted Arthur, backing away. "What's that you said?"

"L-L-L-L-L-L-Listen," vibrated the other.

Still pressing his hands on the hurdle, he leaned upon them until the top part of his body hung perilously over. His face wore an expression of unutterable relief.

"Can't you *hear*," he squeaked, red in the face.

And then Arthur was quite sure about something that he had been vaguely hearing for some moments. It sounded like about a hundred alarum clocks all going off at once, muffled somehow, but concentrated. It was a sort of whirring, low and spasmodic at first, but broadening out into something more regular, less frantic.

"What that noise?" he demanded, thoroughly frightened by now.

"It's only my clock," said the other. He clambered over the hurdle, a little stiffly, as though not quite sure of his limbs. Except for a general awkwardness, an abrupt tremor now and again, he seemed to have become quite rational and ordinary. Arthur scarcely comprehended the remark, and it certainly did not explain the origin of the harassing noise. He gaped at the figure—less strange now, although still puzzling—and noticed for the first time his snuff-coloured suit of rather odd pattern, his boots of curious leaden hue, his podgy face with a snub nose in the middle of it, his broad forehead surmounted by the funny fringe of the wig. His voice, as he went on speaking, gradually increased in pitch until it reached an even tenor.

"Perhaps I ought to explain," he continued. "You see, I'm a clockwork man."

"Oh," said Arthur, his mouth opening wide. And then he stammered quickly, "that noise, you know."

The Clockwork man nodded quickly, as though recollecting something. Then he moved his right hand spasmodically upwards and inserted it between the lapels of his jacket, somewhere in the region of his waistcoat. He appeared to be trying to find something. Presently he found what it was he looked for, and his hand moved again with a sharp, deliberate action. The noise stopped at once. "The silencer," he explained, "I had forgot to put it on. It was such a relief to be working again. I must have nearly stopped altogether. Very awkward. Very awkward, indeed."

He appeared to be addressing the air generally.

"The fact is I need a good overhauling. I'm all to pieces. Nothing seems right. I oughtn't to creak like this. I'm sure there's a screw loose somewhere."

He moved his arm slowly round in a circle, as though to reassure himself. The arm worked in a lop-sided fashion, like a badly shaped wheel, stiffly upwards and then quickly dropping down the curve. Then the Clockwork man lifted a leg and swung it swiftly backwards and forwards. At first the leg shot out sharply, and there seemed to be some difficulty about its withdrawal; but after a little practice it moved quite smoothly. He continued these experiments for a few moments, in complete silence and with a slightly anxious expression upon his face, as though he were really afraid things were not quite as they should be.

Arthur remained in stupefied silence. He did not know what to make of these antics. The Clockwork man looked at him, and seemed to be trying hard to remould his features into a new expression, faintly benevolent. Apparently, however, it was a tremendous effort for him to move any part of his face; and any change that took place merely made him look rather like a caricature of himself.

"Of course," he said slowly, "you don't understand. It isn't to be expected that you would understand. Why, you haven't even got a clock! That was the first thing I noticed about you."

He came a little nearer to Arthur, walking with a hop, skip and jump, rather like a man with his feet tied together.

"And yet, you look like an intelligent sort of being," he continued, "even though you are an anachronism."

Arthur was not sure what this term implied. In spite of his confusion he couldn't help feeling a little amused. The figure standing by his side was so exactly like a wax-work come to life, and his talk was faintly reminiscent of a gramophone record.

"What year is it?" enquired the other suddenly, and without altering a muscle of his face.

"Nineteen hundred and twenty-three," said Arthur smiling faintly.

The Clockwork man lifted a hand to his face, and with some difficulty lodged a finger reflectively against his nose. "Nineteen hundred and twenty-three," he repeated, "that's interesting. Very interesting, indeed.

Not that I have use for time, you know."

He appeared to ruminate, still holding a finger against his nose. Then he shot his left arm out with a swift, gymnastic action and laid the flat palm of his hand upon Arthur's shoulder.

"Did you see me coming over the hill?" he enquired.

Arthur nodded.

"Where did you think I came from?"

"To tell the truth," said Arthur, after a moment's consideration, "I thought you came out of the sky."

The Clockwork man looked as though he wanted to smile and didn't know how. His eyes twinkled faintly, but the rest of his face remained immobile, formal. "Very nearly right," he said, in quick, precise accents, "but not quite."

He offered no further information. For a long while Arthur was puzzled by the movements that followed this last remark. Apparently the Clockwork man desired to change his tactics; he did not wish to prolong the conversation. But, in his effort to move away, he was obviously hampered by the fact that his hand still rested upon Arthur's shoulder. He did not seem to be able to bend his arm in a natural fashion. Instead, he kept on making a half-right movement of his body, with the result that every time he so moved he was stopped by the impingement of his hand against Arthur's neck. At last he solved the problem. He took a quick step backwards, nearly losing his balance in the process, and cleared his arm, which he then lowered in the usual fashion. Then he turned sharply to the left, considered for a moment, and waddled away. There was no other term in Arthur's estimation, to describe his peculiar gait. He took no stride; he simply lifted one foot up and then the other, and then placed them down again slightly ahead of their former positions. His body swayed from side to side in tune with his strange walk. After he had progressed for a few yards he turned to the right, with a smart movement, and looked approximately in Arthur's direction. His mouth opened and shut very rapidly, and there floated across the intervening space some vague and very unsatisfactory human noise, obviously intended as an expression of leave-taking. Then he turned to the left again, with the same drill-like action, and waddled along.

IV

Arthur watched him, feeling diffident, half inclined to follow him in case he fell over. For there was not much stability about the Clockwork man. It was clear the slightest obstacle would have precipitated him upon his nose. He kept his head erect, and looked neither downwards or to right and left. He seemed wholly absorbed in his eccentric mode of locomotion, as though he found it interesting just to be moving along. Arthur kept his eyes glued upon that stiff, upright back, surmounted by the wig and hat, and he wondered what would happen when the Clockwork man reached to the end of the line of hurdles, where another barrier started at right angles across the end of the cricket ground.

It was a sight to attract attention, but fortunately, as Arthur thought, everyone seemed too absorbed in the game to notice what was happening. The dawning of humour saved him from some uncomfortable misgivings. There was something uncanny about the experience. Somehow, it didn't seem natural, but it was certainly funny. It was grotesque. You had to laugh at the odd-looking figure, or else feel cold all over with another kind of sensation. Of course, this man was mad. He was, in spite of his denial, an escaped lunatic. But the noise? That was certainly difficult to explain. Perhaps he had some kind of infernal machine hidden in his pocket, in which case he would be a dangerous kind of lunatic.

What was he going to do next? He had reached to the end of the field and stopped abruptly. Apparently, the presence of another barrier acted as a complete check to further movement. For several seconds he remained perfectly still. He was now about a hundred yards from Arthur, but the latter had good eyesight, and he was determined to miss nothing.

Then the Clockwork man raised a hand slowly to his face, and Arthur knew he was repeating his former meditative action, finger to nose. He remained in that position for another minute, as though the problem of which way to turn was almost too much for him. Finally, he turned sharp to the right and began to walk again.

Arthur became aware of two other figures approaching the one he was watching so intently. They were Gregg, the captain of the team, and

Doctor Allingham. The yellow braid on their blazers shone in the sunlight, and Arthur could see the blue emblem on Gregg's pocket. There would have to be a meeting. The two flannelled figures were strolling along in a direct line towards that other oddly insistent form. Arthur caught his breath. Somehow he dreaded that encounter. When he looked again there was some kind of confabulation going on. Curiously enough, it was Doctor Allingham and Gregg who seemed incapable of movement now. They stood there, with their hands in their pockets, staring, listening. But the Clockwork man was apparently making the utmost use of his limited range of action. His arms were busy. Sometimes he kicked a leg up, as though to emphasise some tremendously important point. And now and again he jabbed a finger outwards in the direction of the field of play. Arthur caught the sound of a high, squeaky voice borne upon the light breeze.

Whatever the argument was about, the Clockwork man seemed to gain his point, for presently the three figures turned together and proceeded in a bee-line towards the pavilion, Doctor Allingham and Gregg dodging about absurdly in their effort to accommodate themselves to the gyrations of their companion.

CHAPTER 2
The Wonderful Cricketer

I

"WE OUGHT NOT to have let him play," said Allingham irritably. He was standing beside Gregg in the pavilion.

"Well, he would insist," said the latter, laughing lightly, "and we're at least entitled to put eleven men in the field. There he goes again! That's a six for certain."

Allingham watched the ball disappear, for the fourth time since the Clockwork man started his inning, somewhere in the direction of a big brewery that stood mid-way between the ground and the distant town. It was an incredible hit. No one had ever achieved such colossal drives in all the history of Great Wymering cricket. There was a certain absurdity about the thing. Already the club had been obliged to supply three extra balls, for it would have been useless to try and find those that had been lifted so far beyond the ground.

"The man's a dangerous lunatic," asserted Allingham, who had not yet overcome his original annoyance with the strange figure, whose sudden advent had lost him his wicket. "It's uncanny, this sort of thing. You can't call it cricket."

"Well, he's making runs, anyhow," rejoined Gregg, his eye falling upon the score-board. "At this rate we shall stand a chance after all."

It was fortunate, perhaps, that the Great Wymering people took their cricket rather seriously. Otherwise, they might have felt, as Doctor Allingham already felt, that there was something impossible about the Clockwork man's performance. He had walked out to the wicket amidst comparative indifference. His peculiar gait might easily have been attributed to sheer nervousness, and his appearance, without flannels, provoked only a slight degree of merriment. When he arrived at the wicket he paused and examined the stumps with great attention, as though wondering what they were for; and it was quite a little while before he arranged himself in the correct attitude before them. He remained standing still, holding the bat awkwardly in the air, and no amount of persuasion on the part of the umpire could induce him to take center or place his bat to the ground in the recognized fashion. He offered no explanation for his eccentric behavior and the fact simply had to be accepted.

The game restarted. Tanner, who by this time had taken eight wickets for just under a hundred runs, put down a slow, tricky one. Everybody agreed, in discussing the matter afterwards, that the Clockwork man never shifted his position or moved a muscle until the ball pitched, slightly to the off. Nobody seems to have seen exactly what happened, but there was a sudden ear-piercing crack and a swoop of dust.

Some seconds elapsed before anyone realised that the ball had been hit at all. It was the Clockwork man who drew attention to the fact by gazing upwards in the direction of the town. And then, suddenly, everybody was straining their eyes in the same direction to watch that little flying spot grow smaller and smaller until it seemed to merge into space. (As a matter of fact, this particular ball was discovered, three weeks later, lying in a disused yard three miles from the cricket ground.)

There was a certain amount of applause followed by an embarrassing silence. Presently someone threw another ball out into the field, and the game was resumed. But the Clockwork man treated Tanner's next delivery, which was a fast one, in exactly the same manner. Again nobody could say exactly what happened—for the action was swifter than the quickest eye could follow—but the ball disappeared again, this time in the direction of a fringe of poplars far away on the horizon. Again there was a lull but the applause this time was modified. Another ball was supplied, and this also was dispatched with equal force and in a third direction, almost unanimously decided by the bewildered spectators to be flagstaff of the church that stood in the middle of High Street, Great Wymering.

By this time a certain sense of panic was beginning to be displayed by the restless attitudes of the fielders; and the spectators, instead of leaning against the barriers, stood about in groups discussing the most extraordinary cricketing event of their lives. There was much head shaking and harping back to precedent among the old cronies present, but it was generally agreed that such hitting was abnormal. Indeed, it was something outside the pale of cricket altogether.

"If everybody was to start 'itting like that," pronounced Samuel Bynes, a local expert, "there wouldn't be no sense in cricket. It ain't in the game." And he spat decisively as though to emphasis his opinion that such proficiency should be deplored rather than commended.

"You're right, Sam," said George Bynes, who had hit up many a century for his town in bygone days, "'tain't cricket. Else it's a fluke; the man didn't ought to be allowed to hold a bat in his hands. It's spoiling other folks' sport."

Attention was diverted by something of minor importance, that showed the Clockwork man in an altogether new and puzzling light. There had been some delay over the procuring of the third ball, and when this was forthcoming the over was called. The fielders changed about, but the Clockwork man made no attempt to move and manifested no interest in the immediate proceedings. He remained, with the bat in his hands, as though waiting for another ball to be delivered.

"Seems as though 'e's on'y 'alf there," commented Mr. Bynes, noticing this incident.

"Dreaming like," suggested his companion.

There was further delay. The bowler at the other end objected to the position of the Clockwork man. He argued, reasonably enough, that the non-participating batsman ought to stand quite clear of the wicket. The umpire had to be consulted, and, as a result of his decision, the Clockwork man was gently but firmly induced to move further away. He then remained, in the same attitude, at the extreme edge of the crease. His obtuseness was certainly remarkable, and comment among the spectators now became general and a trifle heated.

"Play," said the umpire.

The batsman at the other end was a stout, rather plethoric individual. He missed the first two balls, and the third struck him full in the stomach. There was a sympathetic pause whilst Mr. Bumpus, who was well known and respected in the town, rubbed this rather prominent part of his anatomy to the accompaniment of fish-like gaspings and excusable ejaculations. Mr. Bumpus was middle-aged and bald as well as corpulent, and although he did his best to endure the mishap with sportsman-like stoicism, the dismay written upon his perspiring features was certainly an excitant to mirth. Some of the fielders turned their heads for a few moments as though to spare themselves a difficult ordeal; but on the whole there was discreet silence.

It was for this reason, perhaps, that the action of the Clockwork man was all the more noticeable. To this day, not one of the persons present is certain as to whether or not this eccentric individual actually did laugh; but everybody is sure that such was his intention. There issued from his mouth, without a moment's warning, a series of harsh, metallic explosions, loud enough to be heard all over the ground. One compared the noise to the ringing of bells hopelessly cracked and out of tune. Others described it as being similar to the sound produced by some person passing a stick swiftly across an iron railing. There was that suggestion of rattling, of the impingement of one hard thing against another, or the clapping together of steel plates. It was a horrible, discordant sound, brassy and resonant, varied between louder outbursts by a sort of whirring and humming. Those who ventured to look at the Clockwork man's face during this extraordinary performance said that there was little change of expression. His mouth had opened slightly, but the laugh, if indeed it could be described as anything but a lugubrious travesty of human mirth, seemed to proceed from far down within him. And then the hideous clamour stopped as abruptly as it began. The Clockwork man had not altered his position during the proceedings; but Arthur Withers, who was watching him with feverish intensity from the pavilion, fancied that his ears flapped twice just after the noise had subsided.

It was an unpleasant episode, but fortunately the object of such misplaced and ugly hilarity scarcely seemed to notice the outrage. Mr. Bumpus was not lacking in courage. After a few more groans and sighs, and a final rubbing of that part of him that had been injured, he placed himself in preparation to receive the next ball. The spectators loudly applauded him, and the bowler, perhaps unwilling to risk another misadventure, moderated his delivery. Mr. Bumpus struck the ball lightly, and it sped away through the slips. A fielder darted after it, but there was ample time for a run. "Come on!" shouted Mr. Bumpus, and started to puff and blow his way down the pitch.

But the Clockwork man paid not the slightest heed to the command. He remained, statuesque, a figure of gross indifference. Mr. Bumpus pulled himself up sharply, midway between the two wickets; his red face was a study of bewilderment. He slid a few paces, cast one imploring glance in the direction of the Clockwork man, and then rushed desperately back to his own crease. But he was too late; his wicket had been put down.

Etiquette plays an important part in the noble game of cricket. It may be bad form to refuse an obvious run; but to complain to your partner in public is still worse. Besides, Mr. Bumpus was too aghast for speech, and his stomach still pained him. He walked very slowly and with great dignity back to the pavilion, and his annoyance was no doubt amply soothed by the loud cheers that greeted his return. Gregg came out to meet him, with a rather shamefaced smile upon his features.

"I'm sorry," he murmured, "our recruit seems to be awkward. I don't think he quite understands."

"He can hit," said Mr. Bumpus, mopping his brow, "but he's certainly an eccentric sort of individual. I called to him to run, and apparently he did not or *would* not hear me."

Gregg caught hold of Arthur Withers, who was just going to bat. "Look here," he said, "just tell our friend that he must run. I don't think he quite grasps the situation."

"No," said Arthur slowly. "I don't think he does. He's rather a peculiar sort of person. I—I—spoke to him. He—he—says he's a clockwork man."

"Oh," said Gregg, and his face became blank. "Anyhow, just tell him that he must run when called."

Arthur walked out to the wicket. His usual knee-shaking seemed less pronounced, and he felt more anxious about the Clockwork man than about himself. He paused as he drew near to him, and whispered in an ear—rather fearfully, for he dreaded a recurrence of the ear-flapping business. "The captain says will you run, please, when you are asked."

The Clockwork man turned his head slightly to the right, and his mouth opened very wide. But he said nothing.

"You have to run," repeated Arthur, in louder tones.

The other flapped an ear. Arthur hastened away. Nothing was worth while risking an exhibition in public such as he had witnessed in comparative seclusion. He supposed there was something about the Clockwork man really phenomenal, something that was beyond his own rather limited powers of comprehension. Perhaps cleverer people than himself might understand what was the matter with this queer being. He couldn't.

He took his place at the wicket. The first ball was an easy one, and he managed to hit it fair on and square to mid-on. Scarcely hoping for response, he called to the Clockwork man and began to run. To his immense astonishment, the latter passed him halfway down the pitch, his legs jumping from side to side, his arms swinging round irresponsibly. It might be said that his run was merely an exaggeration of his walk. Arthur dumped his bat down quickly, and turned. As he looked up, on the return journey, he was puzzled by the fact that there was no sign of his partner. He paused and looked around him.

There had been an outburst of derisive cheering when the Clockwork man actually commenced to run, but this now swelled up into a roar of merriment. And the Arthur saw what had happened. The Clockwork man had not stopped at the opposite wicket. He had run straight on, past the wicket-keeper, past the fielders, and at the moment when Arthur spotted him he was making straight for the white sheet at the back of the ground. No wonder the crowd laughed! It was so utterly absurd; and the Clockwork man ran as though nothing could stop him, as though, indeed, he had been wound up and was without power to check his own ridiculous progress. The next moment he collided with the sheet; but even this could only prevent him from going further. His legs continued to work rapidly with the action of running, whilst his body billowed into the sagging sheet.

The spectators gave themselves up wholly to the fun. It must have seemed to them that this extraordinary cricketer was also gifted with a sense of humour, however eccentric; and that this nonsensical action was intended by way of retaliation for the ironic cheers that had greeted his running at all. Nobody, except Arthur Withers, realised that the Clockwork man had run thus far because for some reason he had been unable to stop himself. It may be remarked here that many of the Clockwork man's subsequent performances had this same accidental air of humour; and that even his most grotesque attitude gave the observer an impression of some wild practical joke. He was so far human, in appearance and manner, in spite of those peculiar internal arrangements, which will be dealt with later, that his actions produced an instantaneous appeal to the comic instinct; and in laughing at him people forgot to take him seriously.

But Arthur Withers, still feeling a certain sense of duty towards that helpless figure battening himself against the sheet, ran up to him. He decided it would be useless to try and explain matters. The Clockwork man was obviously quite irresponsible. Arthur laid his hands on his shoulders and turned him round, much in the way that a child turns a mechanical toy after it has come to rest. Thus released, the running figure proceeded back towards the wicket, followed close at heels by Arthur, who hoped, by means of a push here and a shove there, to guide him back to the pavilion and so out of harm's way.

But in this attempt he was unexpectedly thwarted. The Clockwork man recovered himself; he ran straight back to the wicket and then stopped dead. The umpire was in the act of replacing the bails, for the wicket had been down, and, fast as this eccentric cricketer had run in the first place, he had not been quick enough to reach the crease in time. By all the rules of the game, and beyond the shadow of doubt, he had been "run out." He now regarded the stumps meditatively, with a finger jerked swiftly against his nose, as though recognizing a former state of consciousness. And then, with a swift movement, he took up his position in readiness to receive the ball.

This was too much for the equanimity of the spectators. Shout after shout volleyed along the lines of the hurdles. This calm deliberateness of the Clockwork man, in so reinstating himself, fairly crowned all his previous exhibitions. And the fact that he took no notice of the merriment at his expense, but simply waited for something to happen, permitted the utmost license. The crowd rocked itself in unrestrained hilarity.

But a second later there was stony silence. For the thing that happened next was as unexpected as it was startling. Nobody, save perhaps Dr. Allingham, anticipated that the Clockwork man was capable of adding violence to eccentricity; he looked harmless enough. But apparently there lurked a dæmonic temper behind those bland, meaningless features. The thing happened in a trice; and all that followed occupied but a few catastrophic seconds. The umpire had stepped up to the Clockwork man in order to explain to him that he was expected to retire from the wicket. Not hearing any coherent reply, he emphasized his request by placing a hand suggestively on the other's shoulder. Instantly, something blade-like flashed in the stammering air, a loud thwack broke upon the silence, and the unfortunate umpire lay prostrate. He had gone down like a log of wood.

Pandemonium ensued. The scene of quiet play was transformed into a miniature battlefield. The fielders rushed in a body at the Clockwork man, only to go down one after the other, like so many ninepins. They lay, stunned and motionless. The Clockwork man spun round like a teetotum, his bat flashing in the sun, whilst the flannelled figures flying from all parts of the field approached him, only to be sent reeling and staggering to earth. Some dodged for a moment only to be caught on the rebound. Dust flew up, and to add to the whirl and confusion the unearthly noise that had startled Arthur Withers broke out again, with terrific force, like the engine of a powerful motor suddenly started.

"I told you he was mad!" shouted Allingham, as he and Gregg leapt through the aperture of the pavilion and dashed to the rescue.

But the Clockwork man suddenly seemed panic-stricken. Just for one moment he surveyed the prostrate figures lying about on the grass like so many sacks. Then he sent the bat flying in the direction of the pavilion and rushed straight for the barrier of hurdles.

The spectators fled with one accord. Allingham and Gregg doubled up in hot pursuit. Arthur Withers, who had mustered the wit to fall down rather than to be knocked down, picked himself up quickly and joined them.

"It's alright," he gasped, "He—he—won't be able to climb hurdles."

But there was no accounting for the activities of the Clockwork man. At a distance of about a yard from the ground, his whole body took off from the ground, and he literally floated in space over the obstacle. It was not jumping; it was more like flying. He landed lightly upon his feet, without the least difficulty; and, before the onlookers could recover from their amazement, this extraordinary personage had shot like a catapult, straight up the path along which he had traveled so precariously half an hour before. In a few seconds his diminutive figure passed into the horizon, leaving a faint trail of dust and the dying echo of that appalling noise.

"My God," exclaimed Gregg, grasping a hurdle to steady himself, "It's—it's—incredible."

Allingham couldn't say a word. He stood there panting and swallowing quickly. Arthur Withers caught up to them.

"He—he—goes by machinery, sir. He's a clockwork man."

"Don't be a damned fool," the doctor burst out, "you're talking through you're hat."

Gregg was listening very acutely.

"But it *is so*," protested Arthur. "you didn't see him as I did. He was like nothing on earth—and then he began to work. Just like a motor starting. And then that noise began. I'm sure there's something inside him, something that goes wrong sometimes."

He was still a little sorry for the Clockwork man.

"That's my conviction," he gasped out, too excited and breathless for further speech.

"I think," said Gregg, with curious calmness, "I think we had better warn the police. He's likely to be dangerous."

CHAPTER 3
The Mystery of the Clockwork Man

I

AN HOUR AND a half later Doctor Allingham and Gregg had their tea together in the sitting room of the former's residence. Bay windows looked out upon the broad High Street, already thronged with Saturday evening excursionists. An unusually large crowd was gathered around the entrance to the "Blue Lion," just over the way, for the news had soon spread about the town. Wild rumours passed from ear to ear as to the identity of the strange individual whose behavior had resulted in so disturbing a conclusion of the cricket match. Those among the townspeople who had actually witnessed not only this event but also the rapid flight of the Clockwork man, related their version of the affair, adding a little each time and altering their theories, so that in the end those who listened were more frightened and impressed than those who had seen.

Allingham sat in a stony silence, sipping tea at intervals and cutting pieces of cake into neat little squares, which he slipped into his mouth spasmodically. Now and again he passed a hand across his big tawny moustache and pulled it savagely. His state of tense nervous irritation was partly due to the fact that he had been obliged to wait so long for his tea; but he had also violently disagreed with Gregg in their discussion about the Clockwork man. At the present moment the young student stood by the window, watching the animated crowd outside the inn. He had finished his tea, and he had no wish to push his own theory about the mysterious circumstance to the extent of quarrelling with his friend.

After the disaster there had been much to do. Four times had Allingham's car traveled between cricket ground and the local hospital, and it was half past six before the eleven players and the two umpires had been conveyed thither, treated for their wounds and discharged. No one was seriously injured, but in each case the abrasion on the side of the head had been severe enough to demand treatment. One or two had a long while recovering full consciousness, and all were in a condition of mental confusion and gave wildly incoherent reports of the incident.

There had been times, during those journeys to and fro, when Gregg found it difficult to save himself from outbursts of laughter. He had to bite his lip hard in the effort to hold in check an imagination that was apt to run to extremes. From one point of view it had certainly been absurd that this awkward being, with his apparently limited range of movement, should have managed in a few seconds to lay out so many healthy, active men. By comparison, his battling performance, singular as it had seemed, faded into insignificance. The breathless swiftness of the action, the unerring aim, the immense force behind each blow, the incredible audacity of the act, almost persuaded Gregg that the thing was too exquisitely comic to be true. But when he forced himself to look at the matter seriously, he felt that there were little grounds for the explanation that the Clockwork man was simply a dangerous lunatic. The flight at preposterous speed, the flying leap over the hurdle, the subsequent acceleration of his run to a pace altogether beyond human possibility, convinced the young undergraduate, who was level-headed enough, although impressionable, that some other explanation would have to be found for the extraordinary occurrence.

Besides, there was Arthur Wither's story about the flapping ears and the queer conversation of the Clockwork man, his peculiar jerky movements, his sudden exhibitions of uncanny efficiency contrasted with appalling lapses. Once you had grasped the idea of his mechanical origin, it was difficult to thrust the Clockwork man out of your head. He became something immensely exciting and suggestive. If Gregg's sense of humour had not been so violently tickled by the ludicrous side of the affair, he would have felt already that some great discovery was about to be revealed to the modern world. It had never occurred to him before that abnormal phenomena might be presented to human beings in the form of a sort of practical joke. Somehow, one expected this sort of thing to happen in solemn earnest and in the dead of night. But the event had taken place in broad daylight, and already there was mixed up with its queer unreality the most ridiculous tangle of purely human circumstance.

Allingham had an explanation for everything. He said that the loud noise was due to some kind of machine that this ingenious lunatic carried in his pocket. He argued that the rapid flight was probably to be accounted for by a sort of electric shoe. Nothing was impossible so long as you could adduce some explanation that was just humanly credible. And the strange antics of the Clockwork man, his sudden stoppings and beginnings, his "Anglo-Saxon" gestures and his staccato gait, all came under the heading of locomotor ataxia in an advanced form.

As the doctor concentrated upon a delayed tea, his mind lapsed into its usual condition of fretful scepticism. Gregg's idea that the Clockwork man represented a mystery, if not a miracle, enraged him. At forty a man does not readily welcome discoveries that may upset his own world of accepted facts, and Allingham had long since given up the habit of following the latest results of scientific investigation. Years ago he had made his own small researches, only to discover that others were making them at the same time. He had had his gleamings in common with all the other students of his year. Everybody was having gleamings then of vast possibilities in medical science, especially in the direction of nervous pathology and the study of morbid diseases resulting from highly complex methods of living. There had been much sound work, a good deal of irresponsible mud-raking, and, in Allingham's case, a growing suspicion that the human organism was not standing very well the strains imposed upon it by modern civilization. He wondered then if some experiments would not be made some day in the pursuit of evolutionary doctrines as applied to physiological progress—but that had been the most ephemeral of all his gleams.

He had been glad to abandon the hospitals in favour of a comfortable practice and the leisured life of a country town. Great Wymering had offered him plenty of distractions that soothed the slight wound to his vanity caused by the discovery that he had over-estimated his originality. In a few years much had happened that helped to confirm his new view of himself as a social creature with a taste for the amenities of existence. And then he had been able to keep up his cricket. In the winter there were bridge parties, amateur theatricals, dinner parties with quite ordinary people, local affairs into which a man whose health was under suspicion and whose sympathies were just perceptibly narrowing, could plunge without too much effort being required in order to rise to such occasions. And he had the witty temperament. Quite easily, he maintained a reputation for turning out a bonmot on the spur of the moment, something with a faint element of paradox. He would say such things as, "Only those succeed in life who have brains and can forget the fact," or "To be idle is the goal of all men, but only the industrious achieve it." When taunted by a young lady who suspected him of wasted talents, even genius, he retorted that "Genius is only an accumulation of neglected diseases."

Latterly he had suffered from strange irritations not easily to be ascribed to liver, misgivings, a sense of having definitely accepted a secondary edition of himself. An old acquaintance would have detected at once the change in his character, the marked leaning towards conservatism in politics and a certain reactionary tendency in his general ideas. He was becoming fixed in his views, and believed in a stable universe. His opinions, in fact, were as automatic as his Swedish exercises in the morning and his apple before breakfast. There was a slight compensatory increase in his sense of humour, and there was his approaching marriage to Lilian Payne, the gifted daughter of a wealthy town councillor.

The last fact occupied a central place in his mind just at present, but it was also another source of irritation. Lilian was intellectual as well as fascinating, and the former attribute became more marked as they grew more intimate. Instead of charming little notes inviting him to tea he now received long, and, he was obliged to admit, quite excellent essays upon the true place of woman in modern life. He was bound to applaud, but such activity of mind was by no means to his taste. He liked a woman to have thoughts; but a thinking woman was a nuisance.

All these clamouring reforms represented to him merely a disinclination to bother about the necessary affairs of life, an evasion of inevitable evils, a refusal to accept life as a school of learning by trial and error. Besides, if women got hold of the idea of efficiency there would be an end to all things. They would make a worse muddle of the "mad dream" than the men. Women made fewer mistakes and they were temperamentally inclined towards the pushing of everything that they undertook to the point of violent and uncomfortable success.

Efficiency! How he hated the word! It reminded him of his own heartbreaking struggles, not only with the difficulties of an exacting science, but with the complexities of the time in which his youth had been spent, a time when all the intelligent young men had been trying to find some way out of the social evils that then existed—and still existed, as an ironical memorial to their futile efforts. In those days one scarcely dared to move in intellectual circles without having evolved one's personal solution of the social problem, an achievement that implied a great deal of hard reading, attendance at Fabian meetings, and a certain amount of voluntary thinking.

If necessary, one could brush all that up again. How different life was, when it came to be lived; how unlike the sagacious prognostications of doubting youth! There was a substratum underneath all that surge of enquiry and inquisitiveness, all that worry and distress; and that was life itself, known and valued, something that one clung to with increasing strength. The mind grew out of its speculative stage and settled down to a careful consideration of concrete existence.

And then, with a sharp jar, his thoughts reverted to the consideration of another irritating circumstance, this ridiculous Clockwork man, in whom Gregg believed even to the extent of thinking it worth while stating the case for the incredible before a man years his senior in experience and rational thought.

II

Allingham got up and stood behind Gregg at the window. The latter raised his head a little as though to catch any words that might float across from the babel of excited voices opposite. But there was nothing clearly distinguishable.

"You see," said Allingham, nodding his head and wiping his moustache with a handkerchief, "let the thing work on your mind and you ally yourself with these town gossips. They'll talk this affair into a nine days wonder."

Gregg shrugged his shoulders in silence. Presently he looked at his watch. "I wonder if Grey will be back soon." Grey was the local inspector of police, in whose hands they had placed the business of rounding up the Clockwork man. Allingham had loaned out his car for the purpose.

"I doubt if we shall see him before midnight," said the latter. "Even supposing he catches his man before dusk, which is unlikely, it will take him another hour or so to drive to the Asylum."

Gregg failed to suppress an abrupt snigger. He lit a cigarette to cover his confusion. Once more he envisaged that flying figure on the horizon. "At the rate he was going," he remarked, steadily, "and barring accidents, I should say he's reached London by now."

"There will be an accident," retorted Allingham. "Mark my words, he won't get very far."

At that moment Mrs. Masters, the doctor's elderly housekeeper, entered the room in order to clear away the tea things. She was a country woman, given to talking without reserve, except when the doctor's eye fell upon her, as it did upon this occasion. But for once she evaded this check to her natural proclivities; she was not going to be cheated out of her share in the local gossip. She placed the tray on the table and made the visitor an excuse for her loquacity.

"Oh, Mr. Gregg, they say the Devil's come to Great Wymering at last. I'm not surprised to 'ear it, for the goings on in this town 'ave been something terrible since the war. What with the drinking and the young people doing just as they like."

"Have you heard anything fresh?" enquired Gregg, pleasantly.

"Only about old Mr. Winchape," said Mrs. Masters, as she packed the tea things. "He's seen the man that knocked the cricketers down with the bat. That is, if he *is* a man, but they do say—"

"Where did Mr. Winchape see him?" broke in Allingham, abruptly.

"Along the path from Bapchurch, sir." Mrs. Masters moderated her manner before the doctor's searching eye. "Poor old Mr. Winchape, he's not so young as he was, and it did give him a turn. He says he was 'urrying along so as to get 'ome in time for tea, and all of a sudden something flashed by 'im, so quick that he 'ardly realised it. He looked round but it was gone in no time. He reckons it was the Old Man 'imself. There was fire coming out of his mouth and 'is eyes was like two red 'ot coals—"

Allingham stamped his feet on the carpet. "I *will* not listen to such talk, Mrs. Masters! A woman of your age and supposed sense to lend ear to such nonsense. I'm ashamed of you."

Mrs. Masters trembled a little under the rebuke, but she showed no sign of repentance. "I'm only repeating what's said," she remarked. "An' for all I know it might have been the Devil. It says in the Bible that he's to be unbound for a thousand years, and I'm sure he might just as well come here as elsewhere for a start. The place is wicked enough."

"Superstitious nonsense," snorted Allingham. And he continued to snort at intervals while Mrs. Masters hastily collected cups and plates, and retreated with dignity to the kitchen.

"Perhaps you agree with Mrs. Masters?" said Allingham, as soon as the door was closed.

Gregg laughed and lowered himself into an easy chair. "Superstition, after all, is a perfectly legitimate although rudimentary form of human enquiry. These good people want to believe in the Devil. At the least opportunity they evoke his satanic majesty. They are quite right. They are simply using the only material in their minds in order to investigate a mystery."

"A sort of glamour," suggested Allingham, trying to look bored.

"If you like," admitted Gregg, "only it does help them understand, just as all our scientific knowledge helps us to understand the future."

"Why drag in the future," said the other, opening his eyes quickly.

"Because," said Gregg, purposely adopting a monotonous drawl as though to conceal his eagerness, "if my theory is correct, then I assume that the Clockwork man comes from the future."

"It's a harmless enough assumption," laughed Allingham.

Gregg rested his head upon the back of the chair and puffed smoke out. "We will pass over the circumstance of his abrupt appearance at the top of the hill, for it is obvious that he might have come from one of the neighbouring villages, although I don't think he did. You yourself admit that his manner of approach was startling, and that it almost seemed as though he had come from nowhere. But let that be. There are, I admit, as yet few facts in support of my theory, but it is at least significant that one of the first questions he asked should have been, not *where* he was but *when* he was."

"I don't quite follow you," interjected Allingham.

"He asked Arthur Withers what year it was. Naturally, if he did come from the future, his first anxiety would be to know into what period of man's history he had, possibly by some accident, wandered."

"But how could he have come from the future?"

"Time," said Gregg, quickly, "is a relative thing. The future has happened just as much as the past. It is happening at this moment."

"Oh, well, you may be right there," blustered Allingham, "I don't know. I admit I'm not quite up to date in these abstruse speculations."

"I regard that statement of his as highly significant," resumed Gregg, after a slight pause. "For, of course, if the Clockwork man really is, as suggested, a semi-mechanical being, then he could only have come from the future. So far as I am aware, the present has not yet evolved sufficiently even to consider seriously the possibility of introducing mechanical reinforcements into the human body, although there has been tentative speculation on the subject. We are thousands of years away from such a proposition; on the other hand, there is no reason why it should not have already happened outside of our limited knowledge of futurity. It has often occurred to me that the drift of scientific progress is slowly but surely leading us in the direction of some such solution of physiological difficulties. The human organism shows signs of breaking down under the strain of an increasingly complex civilisation. There may be a limit to our power of adaptability, and in that case humanity will have to decide whether it will alter its present mode of living or find instead some means of supplementing the normal functions of the body. Perhaps that has, as I suggest, already happened; it depends entirely upon which road humanity has taken. If the mechanical side of civilization has developed at its present rate, I see no reason why the man of the future should not have found means to ensure his efficiency by mechanical means applied to natural functions."

Gregg sat up in his chair and became more serious. Allingham fidgeted without actually interrupting.

"Imagine an exceedingly complex kind of mechanism," Gregg resumed, "an exaggeration of the many intricate types of modern machine in use to-day. It would have to be something of a very delicate description, and yet rather crude at first in its effect. One thinks of something that would work accurately if in rather a limited sort of way. You see, they would have to ensure success in some things at first even at the sacrifice of a certain general awkwardness. It would be a question of taking one thing at a time. Thus, when the Clockwork man came to play cricket, all he could do was to hit the ball. We have to admit that he did that efficiently enough, however futile were the rest of his actions."

"Hot air," interrupted Allingham, reaching for his tobacco pouch, "that's all this is."

"Oh, I won't admit that," rejoined Gregg, cheerfully, "we must acknowledge that what we saw this afternoon was entirely abnormal. Even when we were talking to him I had a strong feeling come over me that our interrogator was not a normal human being. I don't mean simply his behavior. His clothes were an odd sort of colour and shape. And did you notice his boots? Curious, dull-looking things. As though they were made out of some kind of metal. And then, the hat and wig?"

"You're simply imagining all these things," said Allingham, hotly, as he rammed tobacco into his pipe.

"I'm not. I really noticed them. Of course, I didn't attach much importance to them at the time, but afterwards, when Arthur Withers was telling his story, all that queer feeling about the strange figure came back to me. It took possession of me. After all, suppose he *is* a clockwork man?"

"But what is a clockwork man?" demanded Allingham.

"Well, of course I can't explain that exactly, but the term so obviously explains itself. Damn it, he *is* a clockwork man. He walk, he talks, and behaves exactly as one would imagine—"

"Imagine!" burst out Allingham. "Yes, you can *imagine* such a thing. But you are trying to prove to me that this creature is something that doesn't and can't exist outside your imagination. It won't wash."

"But you agree," said Gregg, unperturbed, "that it might be possible in the future?"

"Oh, well, everything is possible, if you look at it in that light," grudgingly admitted the other.

"Then all we have to do is to prove that the future is involved. Our lunatic must convince us that he is not of our age, that he has, in fact and probably by mechanical means, found his way back to an age of flesh and blood. So far, we are agreed, for I willingly side with you in your opinion that the Clockwork man could not exist in the present; while I am open to be convinced that he is a quite credible invention of the remote future."

He broke off, for at that moment a car drew up in front of the window, and the burly form of Inspector Grey stepped down in company with two constables and a lad of about fifteen, whom both Gregg and the doctor recognised as an inhabitant of the neighbouring village of Bapchurch.

III

"Well?" said Allingham, as the party stamped awkwardly into the room, after a preliminary shuffling upon the mat. "What luck?"

"Not much, doctor," announced the inspector, removing his hat and disclosing a fringe of carroty hair. "We ain't found your man, and so far as I can judge we ain't likely to. But we've found these."

He laid the Clockwork man's hat and wig on the table. Gregg instantly picked them up and began examining them with great curiosity.

"And young Tom Driver here, he's seen the man himself," resumed the inspector. "That's 'ow we come by the 'at and wig. Tell the gentlemen what you saw, Tom."

Tom Driver was a backward youth at the best of times, but he seemed quite overcome by the amount of responsibility now thrust upon him. He shuffled forward, pressing his knees together and holding a tattered cap between his very dirty fingers. A great shock of curly yellow hair fell almost over his large brown eyes, and his face was long and pinched.

"I see the man," he began, timidly, "I see 'im as I was going along the path to Bapchurch."

"Was he going very fast?" said Gregg.

"No, sir, he weren't walking at all. He'd fallen into the chalk pit just by Rock's Bottom."

Allingham burst out into a great roar of laughter; but Gregg merely smiled and listened.

"That's 'ow I come to see 'im," said Tom, shifting his cap about uneasily. "I was in a bit of a 'urry 'cos mother said I wasn't to be late for tea, and I'd been into the town to buy butter as we was a bit short. As I come by Rock's bottom—and you know 'ow the path bends a bit sharp to the left where the chalk pit lies—it's a bit awkward for anyone 'as don't know the path—"

"Yes, go on," said Gregg impatiently.

"Well, as I was coming along I see something moving about just at the top of the pit. At first I thought it was a dog, but when I come nearer I could see it was a pair of legs, kicking. Only they was going so fast you couldn't hardly tell one from t'other. Well, I ran up, thinking 'as very likely someone 'ad fallen in, and sure enough it was someone. I caught 'old of the legs, and just as I was about to pull 'm out—"

"Did the legs go on kicking?" said Gregg, quickly.

"Yes, sir, I 'ad a job to 'old them. And then, just as I was going to pull 'im out, I noticed something—"

Tom paused for a moment and began to tremble. His teeth chattered violently and he looked appealingly at his listeners as though afraid to continue.

"Go on, Tom," commanded Inspector Grey. "Spit it out, lad. It's got to be said."

"He—he—hadn't got no back to his head," blurted out Tom at last.

"What!" rapped out Allingham.

"There you are," said Tom, cowering and glancing reproachfully at the inspector, "I told you as 'ow t' gentlemen wouldn't believe me. T'ain't likely as anybody would believe it as 'adn't seen it for themselves."

"But what did you see?" enquired Gregg, kindly. "What was there to be seen?"

Tom's eyes searched the room as though looking for something. Gregg was standing with his back to the fireplace, but noticing that Tom seemed to be trying to look behind him, he moved away. Tom immediately pointed to the clock that stood on the mantelpiece.

"It was a clock," he said slowly, "just like that one, only more so, in a manner of speaking. I mean it 'ad more 'ands and figures, and they was going round very fast. But it 'ad a glass face just like that one, and it was stuck on 'is 'ead just where the back ought to be. The sun was shining on it at first. That's why I couldn't be sure what it was for a long time. But when I looked closer, I could see plain enough, and it made me feel all wobbly, sir."

"Was there a loud noise?" asked Gregg.

"No sir, not then. But the 'ands was moving very fast, and there was a sort of 'umming going on like a lot of clocks all going at once, only quiet like. I was so taken back I didn't know what to do, but presently I caught 'old of 'is legs and tried to pull 'im out. It weren't a easy job, 'cos 'is legs was kicking all the time, and although I 'ollered out to 'im 'e took no notice. At last I dragged 'im out, and 'e lay on the grass, still kicking. 'E never even tried to get up, and at last I took 'old of his shoulders and picked 'im up. And then as soon as I stood 'im on his feet, and afore I 'ad time to 'ave a good look at 'im, off he goes, like greased lightning. An awful noise started, like machinery, and afore I 'ad time to turn round 'e was down the path towards Bapchurch and out of sight. I tell you, sir, it gave me a proper turn."

"But how did you come by these?" questioned Gregg, who was still holding the hat and wig.

"I see them lying in the pit," explained Tom, "they must've dropped off 'is 'ead as he lay there. Of course, 'e 'adn't fallen very far, otherwise 'is legs wouldn't 'ave been sticking up. It ain't very steep just there, and 'is 'ead must 'ave caught in a bit of furze. But the 'at and wig 'ad rolled down to the bottom. After 'e'd gone I climbed down and picked them up."

Gregg passed the hat and wig to Allingham, and whispered something. The other looked at the inside of the hat. There was a small label in the center, with the following matter printed upon it:—

DUNN BROTHERS.
UNIVERSAL HAT PROVIDERS.
ESTABLISHED OVER 2,000 YEARS.

For a moment Allingham's face was a study in bewilderment. He tried to speak, but only succeeded in producing an absurd snigger. Then he tried to laugh outright, and was forced into rapid speech. "Well, what did I say? The whole thing is preposterous. I'm afraid, inspector, we've troubled you for nothing. The fact is, somebody has been guilty of a monstrous hoax."

"Look at the wig, look at the wig," interrupted Gregg, feverishly.

Allingham did so. Just on the edge of the lining there was an oblong-shaped tab, with small gold lettering:—

W. CLARKSON.
Wig-maker to the Seventh International.

"Well, well, it's what I said," the doctor went on, swallowing quickly, "someone has—someone has—"

He broke off abruptly. Gregg was standing with his hands behind him. He shook his head gravely.

"It's no use, doc," he observed, quietly, "we've got to face it."

CHAPTER 4
Arthur Withers Thinks Things Out

I

AFTER THAT LAST glimpse of the Clockwork man, and the conversation with Doctor Allingham and Gregg that followed, Arthur had hurried home to his tea. No amount of interest in the affair, however stupendous it might appear both to himself and others, could dissuade him from his usual Saturday night's programme. Rose Lomas, to whom he had recently become engaged, was a hundred times more important than a clockwork man, and whether a human being could actually exist who walked and talked by mechanical means was a small problem in comparison with that of changing his clothes, washing and tidying himself up in time for his assignation. As soon as the cricketers showed signs of stirring themselves, and so conveyed the comforting impression that were not dead, Arthur felt himself able to resume normal existence.

His lodgings were situated at the lower end of the town. The accommodation consisted of a small bedroom, which he shared with a fellow clerk, and a place at the table with the other inmates of the house. The street was very dirty, and Mrs. Flack's house alone presented some sign of decency and respectability. It was a two-storied red brick cottage. There was no front garden, and you entered directly into a living room through a door, upon which a brass plate was fixed that bore the following announcement:—

MRS. FLACK
Trained Midwife.

Arthur stumbled into the room, dropped his straw hat on to the broken-down couch that occupied the entire side of one wall, and sat down at the table.

"Well?" enquired Mrs. Flack, as she poured him out a cup of tea, "who won?"

"Nobody," remarked Arthur, cramming bread and butter into his mouth. "Game off."

Mr. Flack, who was seated in his armchair by the fire-place, looked up in amazement. His interest in cricket was immense, but chronic rheumatism prevented him from getting as far as the ground. He was dependent upon Arthur's reports and the local paper.

"'Ow's that, then?" he demanded, slowly.

Arthur swallowed quickly and tried to explain. But, although the affair was still hot in his mind, he found it exceedingly difficult to describe exactly what had taken place. The doings of the Clockwork man were at once obvious and inexplicable. It was almost impossible to intrigue people who had not actually witnessed the affair into a realisation of such extraordinary happenings. Arthur had to resort to abrupt movements of his arms and legs in order to produce an effect. But he made a great point of insistence upon the ear-flapping.

"*Go hon!*" exclaimed Mrs. Flack, leaning her red folded arms upon the table, "well I never!"

"'Tain't possible," objected her husband, "'e's pulling your leg, ma."

But Arthur persisted in his imitations, without caring very much whether his observers believed him or not. It at least afforded an entertaining occupation. Mrs. Flack's motherly bosom rose and fell with merriment. "It's as good as the pictures," she announced at last, wiping her eyes. But when Arthur spoke about the loud noise, and hinted that the Clockwork man's internal arrangements consisted of some kind of machinery, Mr. Flack sat bolt upright and shook his head gravely.

"You're a masterpiece," he remarked, "that's what you are." This was his usual term for anything out of the way. "You ain't a going to get me to believe that, not at my age."

"If you saw him," sad Arthur, emphatically, "you'd *have* to believe. It's just that, and nothing else. He's like one of those mechanical toys come to life. And it's so funny. You'd never guess."

Mr. Flack shook his head thoughtfully. Presently he got up, walked to the end of the mantelpiece, placed his smoked-out pipe on the edge and took an empty one from behind an ornament. Then he returned to his seat and sat for a long time with the empty pipe in his mouth.

"'T'ain't possible," he ruminated, at last, "not for a bloke to 'ave machinery inside 'im. At least, not to my way of thinking."

Arthur finished his tea and got up from his chair. Conscious that his efforts so far had not carried conviction, he spent a few moments of valuable time in an attempt to supplement them.

"He went like this," he explained, imitating the walk of the Clockwork man, and at the same time snapping his fingers to suggest sharp clicking noises. "And the row! Well, you know what a motor sounds like when it's being wound up. Like that, only worse."

Mrs. Flack held the greater part of herself in a semicircle of red arm. "You are a one," she declared. Then she looked at Mr. Flack, who sat unmoved. "Why don't *you* laugh? It would do you good. You take everything so serious."

"I ain't a going to laugh," said Mr. Flack, "not unless I see fit to laugh." And he continued to stare gravely at Arthur's elaborate posturing. Presently the latter remembered his urgent appointment and disappeared through the narrow door that led upstairs.

"Whoever 'e be," said Mr. Flack, referring to the strange visitor to Great Wymering, "I should judge 'im to be a bit of a masterpiece."

II

Upstairs in the bedroom, Arthur hastily removed his flannels and paced the limited amount of floor space between the two beds. What a little box of a place it was, and how absurdly crammed with furniture! You couldn't move an inch without bumping into things or knocking something over. There wasn't room to swing a cat, much less to perform an elaborate toilet with that amount of leisurely comfort necessary to its successful accomplishment. Ordinarily he didn't notice these things; it was only when he was in a hurry, and had all sorts of little duties to carry out, that the awkwardness of his surroundings forced themselves into his mind and produced a sense of revolt. There were times when everything seemed

a confounded nuisance and a chair stuck in your way made you feel inclined to pitch it out of the window. Just when you wanted to enjoy simply
being yourself, when your thoughts were running in a pleasant, easeful
way, you had to turn to dress or undress, shave or wash, prepare yourself
for the conventions of life. So much of existence was spent in actions that
were obligatory only because other people expected you to do the same as
themselves. It wasn't so much a waste of time as a waste of life.

He rescued his trousers from underneath the mattress. It was only
recently that he had discovered this obvious substitute for a trouser press,
and so added one more nuisance to existence. It was something else to be
remembered. He grinned pleasantly at the thought of the circumstance
which had brought about these careful habits. Rose Lomas liked him to
look smart, and he had managed it somehow. There were plenty of dapper
youths in Great Wymering, and Arthur had been astute enough to notice
wherein he had differed from them, in the first stages of his courting. Early
rebuffs had led him to perceive that the eye of love rests primarily upon
a promising exterior, and only afterwards discovers the interior qualities
that justify a wise choice. Arthur had been spurned at first on account of a
slovenliness that, to do him justice, was rather the result of personal conviction, however erring, than mere carelessness. He really had felt that it
was a waste of life even to spend half an hour a month inside a barber's
shop. Not only that, but the experience was far-reaching in its unpleasant consequences. You went into the shop feeling agreeably familiar with
yourself, conscious of intense personality; and you came out a nonentity,
smelling of bay-rum. The barber succeeded in transforming you from an
individual brimming over with original reflections and impulses into a
stranger without a distinctive notion in your head. The barber, in fact, was
a Delilah in trousers; he ravished the locks from your head and bewitched
you into the bargain.

Arthur had a strong sense of originality, although he would have
been the last person to claim originality in his thoughts. He disliked in-
terference with any part of his personal being. As a boy he had been
perturbed by the prospect of growing up. It had seemed to him such

a hopeless sort of process, a mere longitudinal extension, without corresponding gain in other magnitudes. He suspected that other dubious advantages were only to be purchased at the expense of a thinning out of the joys of childhood. Later on, he discovered, sadly enough, that this was the case; although it was possible deliberately to protract one's adolescence. Hence his untidiness, his inefficiency, and even his obtuseness, were less constitutional faults than weapons in the warfare against the encroachment of time.

But the authorities at the bank regarded them as grave defects in his character.

Falling in love had revealed the matter in a very different light. It was quite worthwhile yielding to fashion in order to win the affection of Rose Lomas. And so he had imitated his rivals. He cast aside all ties that revealed their linings, trimmed up the cuffs of his shirts; overcame with an effort a natural repugnance to wearing his best clothes; and generally submitted himself to that daily supervision of superficial matters which he could now regard as the prelude to happy hours. And Rose, interested in that conquest of himself for her sake, had soon learned how much there was beneath the polished surface to capture her heart.

Yes, love made everything different! You were ready to put up with all inconveniences and indignities for the sake of that strange obsession. That thought consoled him as he crept on hands and knees in order to pick up his safety razor that had dropped behind the bulky chest of drawers. Love accounted for everything, both serious and comic.

He found his razor, plunged it into cold water—he had forgotten to ask Mrs. Flack for hot, and couldn't be bothered now—and lathered his face thoughtfully.

How many times, in the course of a life-time, would he repeat that operation? And he would always stand in exactly the same way, with his legs straddled apart, and his elbows spanning out like flappers. He would always pass the razor over his face in a certain manner, avoiding those places where even the sharpest blade boggled a little, proceeding with the same mechanical strokes until the job was once more accomplished. Afterwards, he would laboriously separate the portions of his razor and wipe them methodically, always in the same order. That was because, once you had decided upon the right way to do a thing you adopted that method for good.

He achieved that second grand sweep of the side of his face, ending at the corner of his mouth, and followed it up by a swift upward stroke, annihilating the bristly tuft underneath his lower lip. Looking swiftly at the clock, he noticed that it was getting dreadfully late. That was another curious problem of existence. You were always up against time. Generally, when you had to do something or get somewhere, there was this sense of breathless hurry and a disconcerting feeling that the world ended abruptly at the conclusion of every hour and then began again quite differently. The clock, in fact, was another tyrant, robbing you of that sensation of being able to go on for ever without changing. That was why people said, when they consulted their watches, "How's the enemy?"

He attacked the problem of his upper lip with sturdy resolution. It was important that this part of his face should be quite smooth. There must not be even a suspicion of roughness. Tears started into his eyes as he harrowed that tender surface. He drew in his breath sharply, and in that moment of voluntary and glad travail achieved a metaphysical conception of the first magnitude.

All really important questions in life came under the heading of Time and Space, thought of in capital letters. Recently, he had struggled through a difficult book, in which the author used these expressions a great many times, although in a sense difficult to grasp. Nevertheless, it suddenly became obvious, in a small way, exactly what the chap had been driving at.

And somehow, his thoughts instantly returned to the Clockwork man. He performed the rest of his toilet swiftly, the major part of his brain occupied with reflections that had for their drift the curious ease with which you could perform some operations in life without consciously realising the fact.

III

"Oh, I'm not nearly ready yet!"

Rose Lomas stood at the open window of her bedroom. Her bare arms and shoulders gleamed softly in the twilight. One hand held her loosened hair on the top of her head, and the other pressed a garment to her chest.

"Alright," said Arthur, standing at the gate, "buck up."

Rose looked cautiously around as though to make sure no one else was in a position to observe her *décolleté*. But the road was empty. It seemed pleasant to see Arthur standing there twirling his walking stick and looking upwards at her. She decided to keep him there for a few moments.

"Lovely evening," she remarked, presently.

"Yes, jolly," said Arthur, "buck up."

"*I am* bucking up."

"You're not even dressed!"

"I am," Rose insisted, distantly, "much more than you think. I've got lots on."

They looked solemnly at one another for a long while without even approaching a "stare out."

"How many runs did you make," Rose asked. She had to repeat the question again before he could hear it distinctly. Besides, he never could believe that her interest in cricket was serious.

"None," he admitted, "but I was not out."

Rose considered. "That's not as good as making runs though."

Arthur heard a slight noise somewhere round the back of the cottage. "Someone coming," he warned.

Rose retreated a few steps and lowered her head.

"Walk up the lane," she whispered, "I'll come presently."

"Alright," Arthur nodded, "*buck* up."

He walked a few yards up the road, and then turned through a wicket gate and mounted the hump of a meadow. The narrow path swerved slightly to right and left. Arthur fell to meditating upon paths in general and how they came into existence. Obviously, it was because people always walked in the same way. Countless footsteps, following the same line until the grass wore away. That was very odd when you came to think about it. Why didn't people choose different ways of crossing that particular meadow? Then there would be innumerable paths, representing a variety of choice. It would be interesting to start a path of your own, and see how many people would follow you, even though you deliberately chose a circuitous or not obviously direct route. You could come every day until the path was made.

He climbed over the top of the meadow, descended again into a valley, and stopped before a stile with hedges running away on either side. He decided to wait here for Rose. It would be pleasant to see her coming over the hill.

It was gloaming now. The few visible stars shone with a peculiar individual brightness, and looked strangely pendulous in the fading blue sky. He leaned back and gazed at the depths above him. This time of the day was always puzzling. You could never tell exactly at what moment the sky really changed into the aspect of evening, and then, night. Yet there must be some subtle moment when each star was born. Perhaps by looking hard enough it would be possible to become aware of these things. It would be like watching a bud unfold. Slow change was an impenetrable mystery, for actually things seemed to happen too quickly for you to notice them. Or rather, you were too busy to notice them. Spring was like that. Every year you made up your mind to notice the first blossoming, the initial tinge of green; but always it happened that you awoke one morning and found that some vast change had taken place, so that it really seemed like a miracle.

He sat there, dangling an empty pipe between his teeth. He was not conscious of a desire to smoke, and he felt strangely tolerant of Rose's delay. She would come presently.

Presently his reverie was abruptly disturbed by a faint noise, strangely familiar although remote. It seemed to reach him from the right, as though something crept slowly along the hedge line, hidden from his view. It was a soft, purring sound, very regular and sustained. At first he thought it was the cry of a pheasant, but decided that it was much too persistent. It was something that made a noise in the process of walking along.

He held his breath and turned his head slowly to the right. For a long time the sound increased only very slightly. And then, there broke upon the general stillness a series of abrupt explosions.

Pfft—Pfft—Pfft—Pfft—Pfft—

And the other noise, the purring and whirring, resumed this time so close to Arthur that he instinctively, and half in fear, arose from the stile and looked around him. But the tall hedges sweeping away on either side made it difficult to see anyone who might be approaching under their cover. There was a pause. Then a different sound.

Click—click—clickerty click—clicker clicker—clicker— And so on, becoming louder and louder until at last it stopped, and its place was taken by the dull pitter-patter of footsteps coming nearer and nearer. There was a little harsh snort that might have been intended for a sigh, and then a voice.

"Oh dear, it is trying. It really is most dreadfully trying—"

The next moment the Clockwork man came into full view round the corner of the hedge. He was swaying slightly from side to side, in his usual fashion, and his eyes stared straight ahead of him. He did not appear to notice Arthur, and did not stop until the latter politely stepped aside in order to allow him to pass. Then the Clockwork man screwed his head slowly round and appeared to become faintly apprehensive of the presence of another being. After a preliminary ear-flapping, he opened his mouth very wide.

"You haven't," he began, with great difficulty, "seen a hat and wig?"

"No," said Arthur, and he glanced at the Clockwork man's bald forehead and noticed something peculiar about the construction of the back of his head; there seemed to be some object there which he could not see because they were facing each other. "I'm sorry," he continued, looking rather hopelessly around him, "perhaps we could find them somewhere."

"Somewhere!" echoed the Clockwork man, "that's what seems to me so extraordinary! Everybody says that. The idea of a thing being *somewhere*, you know. Elsewhere than where you expect it to be. It's so confusing."

Arthur consulted his common sense. "Can't you remember the place where you lost them," he suggested.

A faint wrinkle of perplexity appeared on the other's forehead. He shook his head once. "Place. There, again, I can't grasp that idea. What is a place? And how does a thing come to be in one place and not in another?" He jerked a hand up as though to emphasise the point. "A thing either is or it isn't. It can't be in a *place*."

"But it must be somewhere," objected Arthur, "that's obvious."

The Clockwork man looked vaguely distressed. "Theoretically," he agreed, "what you say is correct. I can conceive it as a mathematical problem. But actually, you know, it isn't at all obvious."

He jerked his head slowly round and gazed at the surrounding objects. "It's such an extraordinary world. I can't get used to it at all. One keeps on bumping into things and falling into things—things that ought not to be there, you know."

Arthur could hardly control an eager curiosity to know what the thing was, round and shiny, that looked like a sort of halo at the back of the Clockwork man's head. He kept on dodging from one side to the other in an effort to see it clearly.

"Are you looking at my clock?" enquired the Clockwork man, without altering his tone of speech. "I must apologise. I feel quite indecent."

"But what is it for?" gasped Arthur.

"It's the regulating mechanism," said the other, monotonously, "I keep on forgetting that you *can't* know these things. You see, it controls me. But, of course, it's out of order. That's how I came to be here, in this absurd world. There can't be any other reason, I'm sure." He looked so childishly perplexed that Arthur's sense of pity was again aroused, and he listened in respectful silence.

"You see," the mechanical voice went on, "only about half the clock is in action. That accounts for my present situation." There was a pause, broken only by obscure tickings, regular but thin in sound. "I had been feeling very run down, and went to have myself attended to. Then some careless mechanic blundered, and of course I went all wrong." He turned swiftly and looked hard at Arthur. "All wrong. Absolutely all wrong. And of course, I—I—lapsed, you see."

"Lapsed!" queried Arthur.

"Yes, I lapsed. Slipped, if you like that better—slipped back about eight thousand years, so far as I can make out. And, of course, everything is different." His arms shot up both together in an abrupt gesture of despair. "And now I am confronted with all these old problems of Time and Space."

Arthur's recent reflections returned to him, and produced a little glow in his mind. "Is there a world," he questioned, "where the problems of Time and Space are different?"

"Of course," replied the Clockwork man, clicking slightly, "quite different. The clock, you see, made man independent of Time and Space. It solved everything."

"But what happens," Arthur wanted to know, "when the clock works properly?"

"Everything happens," said the other, "exactly as you want it to happen."

"Awfully convenient," Arthur murmured.

"Exceedingly." The Clockwork man's head nodded up and down with a regular rhythm. "The whole aim of man is convenience." He jerked himself forward a few paces, as though impelled against his will. "But my present situation, you know, is extremely *in*convenient."

He waddled swiftly along, and, to Arthur's great disappointment, disappeared round the corner of the hedge, so that it was impossible to get more than a fleeting glimpse of that fascinating object at the back of his head. But he was still speaking.

"I don't know what I shall do, I'm sure," Arthur heard him say, as though to himself.

IV

Rose Lomas came slowly over the top of the hill. She was hatless, and her short, curly hair blew about her face, for a slight breeze had sprung up in the wake of the sunset. She wore a navy blue jacket over a white muslin blouse with a deep V at the breast. There was a fair stretch of plump leg, stockinged in black cashmere, between the edge of her dark skirt and the beginning of the tall boots that had taken so long to button up. She walked with her chin tilted upwards and her eyes half closed, and her hands were thrust into slanting pockets of her jacket.

"Whoever was that person you were talking to?" she enquired, as soon as they stood together.

"Oh, someone who had lost his way," said Arthur, carelessly. He felt curiously disinclined to explain matters just at present. The Clockwork man was disconcerting. He was a rather terrifying side-issue. Arthur had a feeling that Rose would probably be frightened by him, for she was a timid girl. He half hoped now that this strange being would turn out to be some kind of monstrous hoax.

And so he said nothing. They remained by the stile, courting each other and the silent on-coming of night. They were very ordinary lovers, and behaved just exactly in the same way as other people in the same condition. They kissed at intervals and examined each other's faces with portentous gravity and microscopic care. Leaning against the stile, they were frequently interrupted by pedestrians, some of whom took special care to light their pipes as they passed. But the disturbance scarcely affected them. Being lovers, they belonged to each other; and the world about them also belonged to them, and seemed to fashion its laws in accordance with their desires. They would not have offered you twopence for a reformed House of Commons or an enlightened civilisation.

"Oh, Arthur," said Rose, suddenly, "I want to be like this always, don't you?"

"Yes," murmured Arthur, and then caught his breath sharply. For his ear had detected a faint throbbing and palpitation in the distance. It seemed to echo from the far-off hills, a sort of "chew chew," constantly repeated. And presently, another and more familiar sound aroused his attention. It was the "toot-toot" of an automobile and the jerk of a brake. And then the steady whine of the engine as the car ascended a hill. Perhaps they were pursuing the Clockwork man. Arthur hoped not. It seemed to him the troubles of that strange being were bad enough without there being added to them the persecutions suffered by those to whom existence represents an endless puzzle, full of snares and surprises.

CHAPTER 5
The Clockwork Man Investigates Matters

I

WHATEVER INCONVENIENCES the Clockwork man suffered as a result of having lapsed into a world of strange laws and manifestations, he enjoyed at least one advantage. His power of travelling over the earth at an enormous speed rendered the question of pursuit almost farcical. While Allingham's car sped over the neighbouring hills, the object of the chase returned by a circuitous route to Great Wymering, slowed down, and began to walk up and down the High Street. It was now quite dark, and very few people seemed to have noticed that odd figure ambling along, stopping now and again to examine some object that aroused his interest or got in his way. There is no doubt that during these lesser perambulations he contrived somehow to get the silencer under better control, so that his progress was now muted. It is possible also that his faculties began to adjust themselves a little to his strange surroundings, and that he now definitely tried to grasp his environment. But he still suffered relapses. And the fact that he again wore a hat and wig, although not his own, requires a word of explanation.

It was this circumstance that accounted for the Vicar's late arrival at the entertainment given in aid of the church funds that night. He had lingered over his sermon until the last moment, and then hurried off with only a slight pause in which to glance at himself in the hall mirror. He walked swiftly along the dark streets in the direction of the Templars' Hall, which was situated at the lower end of the town. Perhaps it was because of his own desperate hurry that he scarcely noticed that other figure approaching him, and in a straight line. He swerved slightly in order to allow the figure to pass, and continued on his way.

And then he stopped abruptly, aware of a cool sensation on the top of his head. His hat and wig had gone! Aghast, he retraced his steps, but there was no sign of the articles on the pavement. It seemed utterly incredible, for there was only a slight breeze and he did not remember knocking into anything. He had certainly not collided with the stranger. Just for a moment he wondered.

But duty to his parishioners remained uppermost in the conscientious Vicar's mind, and it was not fair to them that he should catch his death of cold. He hurried back to the vicarage. For a quarter of an hour he pulled open drawers, ransacked cupboards, searching everywhere for an old wig that had been discarded and a new hat that had never been worn. He found them at last and arrived, breathless and out of temper, in the middle of the cinematograph display which constituted the first part of the performance.

"My dear," he gasped, as he slid into the seat reserved for him next to his wife, "I couldn't help it. Someone stole my hat and wig."

"Stole them, Herbert," she expostulated. "Not *stole* them."

"Yes, stole them. I'll tell you afterwards. Is this the Palestine picture? Oh, yes—"

II

And so the Clockwork man was able to conceal his clock from the gaze of a curious world, and the grotesqueness of his appearance was heightened by the addition of a neatly trimmed chestnut wig and a soft round clerical hat. His perceptions must have been extraordinarily rapid, and he must have acted upon the instant. Nor did it seem to occur to him that in this world there are laws which forbid theft. Probably, in the world from which he came such restrictions are unnecessary, and the exigency would not have arisen, every individual being provided by parliamentary statute with a suitable covering for that blatant and too obvious sign of the *modus operandi* in the posterior region of their craniums.

It was shortly after this episode that the Clockwork man experienced his first moment of vivid illumination about the world of brief mortal span.

He had become entangled with a lamp-post. There is no other way of describing his predicament. He came to rest with his forehead pressed against the post, and all his efforts to get round it ended in dismal failure. His legs kicked spasmodically and his arms revolved irregularly. There were intermittent explosions, like the back-firing of a petrol engine. The only person who witnessed these peculiar antics was P.C. Hawkins, who had been indulging in a quiet smoke beneath the shelter of a neighbouring archway.

At first it did not occur to the constable that the noise proceeded from the figure. He craned his head forward, expecting every moment to see a motor bicycle come along. The noise stopped abruptly, and he decided that the machine must have gone up a side street. Then he stepped out of his retreat and tapped the Clockwork man on the shoulder. The latter was quite motionless now and merely leaning against the lamp-post.

"You go 'ome," suggested the constable, "I don't want to have to take you. This is one of my *lenient* nights, lucky for you."

"Wallabaloo," said the Clockwork man, faintly, "Wum—Wum—"

"Yes, we know all about that," said the constable, "but you take my tip and go 'ome. And I don't want any back answers neither."

The Clockwork man emitted a soft whistling sound from between his teeth, and rubbed his nose thoughtfully against the post.

"What *is* this?" he enquired, presently.

"Lamp-post," rejoined the other, clicking his teeth, "L.A.M.P.-P.O.S.T. Lamp-post."

"I see—curious, only one lamp-post, though. In my country they grow like trees, you know—whole forests of them—galaxy of lights—necessary—illuminate multiform world."

The constable laughed gently and stroked his moustache. His theory about the condition of the individual before him slowly developed.

"You get along," he persuaded, "before there's trouble. I don't want to be 'arsh with you."

"Wait," said the Clockwork man, without altering his position, "moment of lucidity—see things as they are—begin to understand—finite world—only one thing at a time. *Now* we've got it—a place for everything and everything in its place."

"Just what I'm always telling my missus," reflected the constable.

The Clockwork man shifted his head very slightly, and one eye screwed slowly round.

"I want to grasp things," he resumed, "I want to grasp *you*. So far as I can judge, I see before me—a constable—minion of the law—curious relic—primitive stage of civilisation—order people about finite world—lock people up—finite cell."

"That's my job," agreed the other, with a warning glint in his red eye.

"Finite world," proceeded the Clockwork man, "fixed laws—limited dimensions—*essentially* limited. Now, when I'm working properly, I can move about in all dimensions. That is to say, in addition to moving backwards and forwards, and this way and that, I can also move X and Y, and X^2 and Y^2."

The corners of the constable's eyes wrinkled a little. "Of course," he ruminated, "if you're going to drag algebra into the discussion I shall 'ave to cry off. I never got beyond decimals."

"Let me explain," urged the Clockwork man, who was gaining in verbal ease and intellectual elasticity every moment. "Supposing I was to hit you hard. You would fall down. You would become supine. You would assume a horizontal position at right angles to your present perpendicularity." He gazed upwards at the tall figure of the constable. "But if you were to hit me, I should have an alternative. I could, for example, fall into the middle of next week."

The constable rubbed his chin thoughtfully, as though he thought this highly likely. "Whatd'yemean by that," he demanded.

"I said next week," explained the other, "in order to make my meaning clear. Actually, of course, I don't describe time in such arbitrary terms, but when one is in Rome, you know. What I mean to convey is that I am capable of going not only somewhere, but also *somewhen*."

"'Ere, stow that gammon," broke in the constable, impatiently, "s'nuff of that sort of talk. You come along with me." He spat determinedly and prepared to take action.

But at that moment, as the constable afterwards described it to himself, it seemed to him that there came before his eyes a sort of mist. The figure leaning against the lamp-post looked less obvious. He did not appear now to be a palpable individual at all, but a sort of shadowy outline of himself, blurred and indistinct. The constable rubbed his eyes and stretched out a hand.

"Alright," he heard a tiny, remote voice, "I'm still here—I haven't gone yet—I *can't* go—that's what's so distressing. I don't really understand your world, you know—and I can't get back to my own. Don't be harsh with me—it's so awkward—between the devil and the deep sea."

"What's up?" exclaimed the constable, startled. "What yer playing at? Where are you?"

"Here I am," the thin voice echoed faintly. The constable wheeled round sharply and became aware of a vague, palpitating mass, hovering in the dark mouth of the archway. It was like some solid body subjected to intense vibration. There was a high-pitched spinning noise.

"'Ere," said the constable, "cut that sort of caper. What's the little game?" He made a grab at where he thought the shadowy form ought to be, and his hand closed on the empty air.

"Gawd," he gasped, "it's a blooming ghost."

He fancied he heard a voice very indistinctly begging his pardon. Again he clutched wildly at a shoulder and merely snapped his fingers. "Strike a light," he muttered, under his breath, "this ain't good enough. It ain't nearly good enough," Reaching forward he stumbled, and to save himself from falling placed a hand against the wall. The next moment he leapt backwards with a yell. His hand and arm had gone clean through the filmy shape.

"Gawd, it's spirits—that's what it is."

"It's only me," remarked the Clockwork man, suddenly looming into palpable form again. "Don't be afraid. I must apologise for my eccentric behaviour. I tried an experiment. I thought I could get back. You said I was to go home, you know. But I can't get far." His voice shook a little. It jangled like a badly struck chord. "I'm a poor, maimed creature. You must make allowances for me. My clock won't work properly."

He began to vibrate again, his whole frame quivering and shaking. Little blue sparks scintillated around the back part of his head. He lifted one leg up as though to take a step forward; and then his ears flapped wildly, and he remained with one leg in mid-air and a finger to his nose.

The constable gave way to panic. He temporised with his duty. "Stow it," he begged, "I can't take you to the station like this. They'll never believe me." He took off his hat and rubbed his tingling forehead. "Say it's a dream, mate," he added, in a whining voice. "'Ow can I go 'ome to the missus with a tale like this. She'll say it's the gin again. It's always my luck to strike something like this. When the ghost came to Bapchurch churchyard, it was me wot saw it first, and nobody believed me. You go along quietly, and we'll look over it this time."

But the Clockwork man made no reply. He was evidently absorbed in the effort to restart some process in himself. Presently his foot went down on the pavement with a smart bang. There followed a succession of sharp explosions, and the next second he glided smoothly away.

The constable returned furtively to his shelter beneath the arch, hitched himself thoughtfully, and found half a cigarette inside his waist-coat pocket.

"It's the gin," he ruminated, half out loud, "I'll 'ave to knock it off. 'Tain't as though I ain't 'ad warnings enough. I've seen things before and I shall see them again—"

He lit the cigarette end and puffed out a cloud of smoke. "I never see 'im," he soliloquised, "not *really*."

III

Perhaps it was the strong glare of light issuing from the half-open door of the Templar's Hall that attracted the attention of the Clockwork man as he wandered along towards the lower end of the town. He entered, and found himself in a small lobby curtained off from the main body of the hall. He must have made some slight noise as he stepped upon the bare boards, for the curtain was swept hastily back, and the Curate, who was acting as chief steward of the proceedings, came hurriedly forward.

As he approached the figure standing beneath the incandescent lamp, the clerical beam upon the Curate's clean-shaven features deepened into a more secular expression of heartfelt relief.

"I'm so glad you have come at last," he began, in a strong whisper,

"I was beginning to be afraid you were going to disappoint us."

"I am certainly late," remarked the Clockwork man, "about eight thousand years late, so far as I can judge."

The Curate scarcely seemed to catch this remark. "Well, I'm glad you've turned up," he went on, "it's so pitiful when the little ones have to be disappointed, and they have been so looking forward to the conjuring. Your things have arrived."

"What things?" enquired the Clockwork man.

"Your properties," said the Curate, "the rabbits and mice, and so forth. They came this afternoon. I had them put on the stage."

He fingered nervously with his watch, and then his eye rested for a second upon the other's head gear.

"Excuse me, but you *are* the conjurer, aren't you?" he enquired, a trifle anxiously.

Before the Clockwork man had time to reply to this embarrassing question, the curtain was again swiftly drawn, and an anxious female face appeared. "James, has the conjurer—Oh, yes, I see he has. Do be quick, James. The picture is nearly over."

The face disappeared, and the Curate's doubts evaporated for the moment. "Will you come this way?" he continued, and led the way through a long, dark passage to the back of the hall. Behind the screen, upon which the picture was being shown, there was a small space, and here a stage had been erected. Upon a small table in the centre stood a large bag and some packages. The Curate adjusted the small gas-jet so as to produce an illumination sufficient to move about. "We must talk low," he explained, pointing to the screen in front of them, "the cinematograph is still showing. We shall be ready in about ten minutes. Can you manage in that time?"

But the Clockwork man made no reply. He stood in the middle of the stage and slowly lifted a finger to his nose. The Curate's doubts returned. Something seemed to occur to him as he examined his companion more closely. "You haven't been taking anything, my good man, have you? Anything of an alcoholic nature?"

"Conjuring," said the Clockwork man, slowly, "obsolete form of entertainment. Quickness of the hand deceives the eye."

"Er—yes," murmured the Curate. He laughed, rather hysterically, and clasped his hands behind his back. "I suppose you do the—er—usual things—gold watches and so forth out of—er—hats. The children have been so looking forward—"

He paused and unclasped his hands. The Clockwork man was looking at him very hard, and his eyes were rolling in their sockets in a most bewildering fashion. There was a long pause.

"Dear me," the Curate resumed at last, "there must be some mistake. You don't look to me like a conjurer. You see, I wrote to Gamages, and they promised they would send a man. Naturally, I thought when you—"

"Gamages," interrupted the Clockwork man, "wait—I seem to understand—it comes back to me—universal providers—cash account—nine and ninepence—nine and ninepence—nine and ninepence—I *beg* your pardon."

"Really!" The Curate's jaw dropped several inches. "I must apologise. You see, I'm really rather flurried. I have the burden of this entertainment upon my shoulders. It was I who arranged the conjuring. I thought it would be so nice for the children." He started rubbing his hands together vigorously, as though to cover up his embarrassment. "Then—then you aren't the man from Gamages?"

"No," said the Clockwork man, with a certain amount of dignity, "I am the man from nowhere."

The Curate's hands became still. "Oh, dear." He wrestled with the blankness in his mind. "You're certainly—forgive me for saying it—rather an odd person. I'm afraid we've both made a mistake, haven't we?"

"Wait," said the Clockwork man, as the Curate walked hesitatingly towards the door, "I begin to grasp things—conjuring—"

"But *are* you the conjurer?" asked the Curate, coming back.

"Where I come from," was the astonishing reply, "we are all conjurers. We are always doing conjuring tricks."

The Curate's hands were busy again. "I really am quite at a loss," he murmured.

"It was a characteristic of the earlier stages of the human race," said the Clockwork man, as though he were addressing a class of students upon some abstruse subject, "that they exercised the arts of legerdemain, magic, illusion and so forth, purely as forms of entertainment in their leisure hours."

"Now that sounds interesting," murmured the Curate, as the other paused, although rather for matter than for breath, "it's so *authoritative*— as though it were a quotation from some standard work. All the same, and much as I should like to hear more—"

"It is a quotation," explained the Clockwork man solemnly, "from a work I was reading when I—when the thing happened to me. It is published by Gamages, and the price is nine and ninepence—nine and ninepence—Oh, bother—"

"I'll make a note of it," said the Curate. "But you must really excuse me now. I have so much to see to. There's the refreshments. The sandwiches are only half cut—"

"It was not until the fifty-ninth century," continued the Clockwork man, speaking with a just perceptible click, "that man became a conjurer in real life. We have here an instance of the complete turning over of human ideas. Ancient man conjured for amusement; modern man conjures as a matter of course, since the invention of the clock and all that its action implies, including the discovery of at least three new dimensions, or fields of action, man's simplest act of an utilitarian nature may be regarded as a sort of conjuring trick. Certainly our forefathers, if they could see us as we are now constituted, would regard them as such—"

"So frightfully interesting," the Curate managed to interpose, "but I really cannot spare the time." He had reverted now to the alcoholic diagnosis.

"The work in question," continued the Clockwork man, without taking any notice at all of the other's impatience, "is of a satirical nature. Its purpose is to awaken people to a sense of the many absurdities in modern life that result from a too mechanical efficiency. It is all in my head. I can spin it all out, word for word—"

"Not now," hastily pleaded the Curate. "Some other time I should be glad to hear it. I am," his mouth opened very wide, "a great reader myself. And of course, as a professional conjurer, your interest in such a book would be two-fold."

"When you asked me if I were a conjurer," said the Clockwork man, "I at once recalled the book. You see, it's actually in my head. That is how we read books now. We wear them inside the clock, in the form of spools that unwind. What you have said brings it all back to me. It suddenly occurs to me that I am indeed a conjurer, and that all my actions in this backward world must be regarded in the light of magic."

The Curate's eyebrows shot up in amazement. "Magic?" he queried, with a short laugh. "Oh, we didn't bargain for magic. Only the usual sleight of hand."

"You see, I had lost faith in myself," said the Clockwork man, plaintively. "I had forgotten what I could do. I was so terribly run down."

"Ah," said the Curate, kindly, "very likely that's what it is. The weather has been very trying. One does get these aberrations. But I do hope you will be able to struggle through the performance, for the children's sake. Dear me, how did you manage to do that?"

The Curate's last remark was rapped out on a sharp note of fright and astonishment, for the Clockwork man, as though anxious to demonstrate his willingness to oblige, had performed his first conjuring trick.

IV

Now the Curate, apart from a tendency to lose his head on occasion, was a perfectly normal individual. There was nothing myopic about him. The human mind is so constituted that it can only receive certain impressions of abnormal phenomena slowly and through the proper channels. All sorts of fantastic ideas, intuitions, apprehensions and vague suspicions had been dancing upon the floor of the Curate's brain as he noticed certain peculiarities about his companion. But he would probably not have given them another thought if it had not been for what now happened.

It would require a mathematical diagram to describe the incident with absolute accuracy. The Curate, of course, had heard nothing about the Clockwork man's other performances; he had scarcely heeded the hints thrown out about the possibility of movement in other dimensions. It seemed to him, in the uncertain light of their surroundings, that the Clockwork man's right arm gradually disappeared into space. There was no arm there at all. Afterwards, he remembered a brief moment when the arm had begun to grow vague and transparent; it was moving very rapidly, in some direction, neither up nor down, nor this way or that, but along some shadowy plane. Then it went into nothing, evaporated from view. And just as suddenly, it swung back into the plane of the curate's vision, and the hand at the end of it grasped a silk hat.

The Curate's heart thumped slowly. "But how did you do it?" he gasped. "And your arm, you know—it wasn't there!"

So far as the Clockwork man's features were capable of change, there passed across them a faint expression of triumph and satisfaction. "I perceive," he remarked, "that I have indeed lapsed into a world of curiously insufficient and inefficent beings. I have fallen amongst the Unclocked. They cannot perceive *Nowhere*. They do not understand *Nowhen*. They lack senses and move about on a single plane. Henceforth, I shall act with greater confidence."

He threw the hat into infinity and produced a parrot cage with parrot.

"Stop it!" the Curate gasped. "My heart, you know—I have been warned—sudden shocks." He staggered to the wall and groped blindly for an emergency exit, which he knew to be there somewhere. He found it, forced the door open and fell limply upon the pavement outside.

The Clockwork man turned slowly and surveyed the prostrate figure. "A rudimentary race," he soliloquised, with his finger nose-wards, "half blind, and painfully restricted in their movements. Evidently they have only a few senses—five at the most." He passed out into the street, carefully avoiding the body. "They have a certain freedom," he continued, still nursing his nose, "within narrow limits. But they soon grow limp. And when they fall down, or lose balance, they have no choice but to embrace the earth."

He waddled along, with his head stuck jauntily to one side. "I have nothing to fear," he added, "from such a rudimentary race of beings."

V

"Evidently," his thoughts ran on, "they must regard me as an extraordinary being. And, of course, *I am*—and far superior. I am a superior being suffering from a nervous breakdown."

He stopped himself abruptly, as though this view of the matter solved a good many problems.

"I must get myself seen to," he mused, "because, of course, that accounts for everything; my lapse into this defunct order of things and my inability to move about freely in the usual, multiform manner. And it accounts for my absurd behaviour just now."

He turned slowly, as though considering whether to return and explain matters to the curate. "I must have frightened him," he whispered, almost audibly, "but I only wanted to show him, and the parrot cage happened to be handy."

He trundled forward again and lurched into the middle of the street.

"Death," he reflected, "that was *death*, I suppose. They still die."

CHAPTER 6

"It was not so, it is not so, and, indeed,
God forbid it should be so."

I

AT THE FOOT of a hill, about five miles from Great Wymering, Doctor Allingham suddenly jammed down the brake of his car, got out, and began pacing the dusty road. Gregg remained seated in the car with his arms folded.

"Aren't you going any further?" he enquired, anxiously.

"No, I'm not," grumbled the Doctor, "I've had enough of this wild-goose chase. And besides, it's nearly dinner time."

"But just now you were inclined to think differently," said Gregg, reproachfully.

"Well, I admit I was rather mystified by that hat and wig. But when you come to rationalise the thing, what is there in it?" The Doctor was taking long strides and flourishing his leather gloves in the air. "How could such a thing be? How can anybody in his right senses entertain the notion that Dunn Brothers are still in existence two thousand years hence? And the Clarkson business. It's absurd on the face of it."

"Even an absurdity," said Gregg, quietly, "may contain the positive truth. I admit it's ludicrous, but we both agree that it's inexplicable. We have to fall back on conjecture. To my mind there is something suggestive about that persistency in the future of things familiar to us. Suppose they have found a way of keeping things going, just as they are? Hasn't the aim of man always been the permanence of his institutions? And wouldn't it be characteristic of man, as we know him to-day, that he should hold on to purely utilitarian things, conveniences? In this age we sacrifice everything to utility. That's because we're getting somewhere in a hurry. Modern life is the last lap in man's race against Time."

He paused, as though to adjust the matter in his mind. "But suppose Time stopped. Or, rather, suppose man caught up with Time, raced the universal enemy, tracked him to his lair? That would account for the names being the same. Dunn still breathes and Clarkson endures, or their descendants. At any rate, the *idea* of them persists. Perhaps this clock that they wear abolished death and successive generations. Of course, it seems like a joke to us, but we've got to drop our sense of humour for the time being."

"But how could it be?" exclaimed Allingham, kicking a loose stone in his walk. "This clock, I mean. It's—" He fumbled hopelessly for words with which to express new doubts. "What *is* this clock?"

"It's an instrument," rejoined Gregg, leaning over the side of the car. "Evidently it has some sort of effect upon the fundamental processes of the human organism. That's clear, to me. Probably it replaces some of the ordinary functions and alters others. One gets a sort of glimmer—of an immense speeding up of the entire organism, and the brain of man developing new senses and powers of apprehension. They would have all sorts of second sights and subsidiary senses. They would feel their way about in a larger universe, creep into all sorts of niches and corners unknown to us, because of their different construction."

"Yes, yes, I can follow all that" said Allingham, biting his moustache, "but let's talk sense."

"In a matter like this," put in Gregg, "sense is at a premium. What we have to do is to consult our intuitions."

Allingham frowned. His intuitions, nowadays, were few and far between.

"When you get to my age, Gregg, you'll have something else to do besides consult your intuitions. The fact is you *want* all these wonderful things to happen. You have a flair for the unexpected, like all children and adolescents. But I tell you, the Clockwork man is a myth, and I think you ought to respect my opinion."

"Even if he's a myth," interrupted Gregg, "he is still worth investigating. What annoys me is your positive antagonism to the idea that he might be possible. You seem to want to go out of your way to prove me in the wrong. I may add, that once a man has ceased to believe in the impossible he is damned."

Allingham shot a look of veiled anger at the other, and prepared to re-enter the car.

"Well, you prove yourself in the right," he muttered, "and then I'll apologise, I'm going to let the Clockwork man drop. I've got other things to think about. And I don't mind telling you that if the Clockwork man turns out to be all that you claim for him, I shall still wish him at the other end of the earth."

"Which is probably where he is now," remarked Gregg, with a slight bantering note in his voice.

"Well, let him stop there," growled Allingham, restarting the car with a vicious jerk, "let someone else bother their heads about him. I don't want him. I tell you I don't care a brass farthing about the future of the human race. I'm quite content to take the good and bad in life, and I want it to go on in the same damned old way."

Gregg beat his fist into his open palm. "But that's just what has happened," he exclaimed, "they've found a way of keeping on just the same. That explains the Clarkson business. If the clock is what I think it is, that precisely is its function."

Allingham shouted out some impatient rejoinder, but it was drowned in the rising roar of the engine as they sped along the road.

II

So the argument had waged since the telling of Tom Driver's story. Gregg's chief difficulty was to get Allingham to see that there really might be something in this theory of a world in which merely trivial things had become permanent, whilst the cosmos itself, the hitherto unchanging outer environment of man's existence, might have opened up in many new directions. Man might have tired of waiting for a so long heralded eternity, and made one out of his own material tools. The Clockwork man, now crystallised in Gregg's mind as an unforgettable figure, seemed to him to stand for a sort of rigidity of personal being as opposed to the fickleness of mere flesh and blood; but the world in which he lived probably had widely different laws, if indeed it had humanly comprehensible laws at all.

The clock, perhaps, was the index of a new and enlarged order of things.

Man had altered the very shape of the universe in order to be able to pursue his aims without frustration. That was an old dream of Gregg's. Time and Space were the obstacles to man's aspirations, and therefore he had invented this cunning device, which would adjust his faculties to some mightier rhythm of universal forces. It was a logical step forward in the path of material progress.

That was Gregg's dimly conceived theory about the mystery, although, of course, he read into the interpretation a good deal of his own speculations. His imagination seized upon the clock as the possible symbol of a new counterpoint in human affairs. In his mind he saw man growing through the ages, until at last, by the aid of this mechanism, he was able to roll back the skies and reveal the vast other worlds that lay beyond, the unthinkable mysteries that lurked between the stars, all that had been sealed up in the limited brain of man since creation. From that extreme postulate it would be necessary to work backward, until some reasonable hypothesis could be found to explain the working of the clock mechanism. That difficulty, even, might be overcome if only an opportunity occurred to examine this strange being from the future, or if he could be prevailed upon to explain matters himself.

As the car sped swiftly along, Gregg sat back with folded arms and gazed upwards at the now crystalline skies, wondering, as he had never wondered before, about that incomprehensible immensity which for centuries of successive generations man had silently respected. No authoritative voice had ever claimed to penetrate that supreme mystery. Priests had evoked the gods from that starry depth, poets had sung of the swinging hemispheres, scientists had traced comets and knew the quality of each solar earth; but still that vast arch spanned all the movements of crawling mankind, and closed him in like a basin placed over a colony of ants.

True, it was an illusion, and man had always known that. For generations he had known that the universe contained more than his limited faculties could perceive. And beauty. There had always been the consoling fact of beauty, lulling the race of man to content, while every now and again a great mind arose and made one more effort to sweep aside the bejewelled splendour that hung between man and his final destiny—to know.

And yet, a slight alteration in man's perceptive organs and that wide blue shell might shatter and disclose a thousand new forms, like fantastic cities shaped in the clouds at sunset. Physiologists claimed that the addition of a single lobe to the human brain might mean that man would know the future as well as the past. What if that miracle had been performed? By such means man might have come to know not only the future, but other dimensions as yet unnamed or merely sketched out by the mathematician in brief, arbitrary terms.

Until that time came, man's deepest speculations about ultimate reality brought him no nearer to the truth than the child worrying himself to sleep over the problem of what happened before God made the universe. Man remained, in that sense, as innocent as a child, from birth to death. Until the actual structure of the cells in his brain suffered a change man could not actually know.

Einstein could say that we were probably wrong in our basic conceptions. But could he say how we were to get right? The Clockwork man might be the beginning.

And then, when that change had been wrought, that physical reconstruction, what else might follow in its train? The Truth at last, an end to all suffering and pain, a solution of the problems of civilisation, such as overpopulation and land distribution, the beginning of human sovereignty in the universe.

But Gregg had the sense to admit to himself that his generalisation was no more than a faint aurora hovering around the rumoured dawn of the future. It was necessary, in the first place, to posit an imperfect thinking apparatus. After all, the Clockwork man was still a mystery to be solved, and even if he failed to justify a single theory born of merely human conjecture, there still remained the exhilarating task of finding out what actually he was and how he had come to earth.

III

Leaving Gregg at his rooms in the upper part of the town, the Doctor drove slowly along the High Street in the direction of his own house. Everything was quiet now, and there was no sign of further disturbance, no indication that a miracle had taken place in the prosaic town of Great Wymering. The Doctor noted the fact with quiet satisfaction; it helped him to simmer down, and it was necessary, for the sake of his digestion, that he should feel soothed and comforted.

Still, if Gregg's conjectures were anywhere near the mark, in a very few hours it would be known all over England that the jaws of the future had opened and disclosed this monstrosity to the eyes of the present. There would be a great stir of excitement; the newspapers would be full of the event. Indeed, the whole course of the world might be altered as a result of this astounding revelation.

He would be dragged into the affair. In spite of himself, he would be obliged to go into some sort of witness box and declare that from the first he had thought the Clockwork man phenomenal, when, as a matter of fact, he had merely thought him a nuisance. But, as one of those who had first seen the strange figure on the hill, and as a medical man, he would be expected to make an intelligent statement. One had to be consistent about such things.

And the real truth was that he had no desire to interest himself in the matter. It disturbed his mental equilibrium, and threatened the validity of that carefully considered world of assumptions which enabled him to make light, easy jests at its inconsistencies and incongruities.

Besides, it was distressing to discover that, in middle life, he was no longer in the vanguard of human hopes and fears; but a miserable backslider, dating back to the time when thought and serious living had become too difficult for comfort. Regarded in this way, nothing could ever compensate for the wasted years, the ideals extinguished, the rich hopes bargained for cheap doubts—unless, indeed, it was the reflection that such was the common lot of mankind. The comfortable old world rolled on from generation to generation, and nothing extraordinary happened to startle people out of their complacent preoccupation with passions, desires and ambitions. Miracles were supposed to have happened at certain stages in world-history, but they were immediately obliterated by a mass of controversial comment, or hushed up by those whose axes were ground in a world that could be relied upon to go on repeating itself.

A comfortable world! Of course, there were malcontents. When the shoe pinched, anybody would cry out for fire from heaven. But if a plebiscite were to be taken, it would be found that an overwhelming majority would be in favour of a world without miracles. If, for example, it could be demonstrated that this Clockwork man was a being in many ways superior to the rest of mankind, he would be hounded out of existence by a jealous and conservative humanity.

But the Clockwork man was not. He never had been, and, indeed, God forbid he ever should be.

With that reflection illuminating his mind, the Doctor ran his car into the garage, and with some return of his usual debonair manner, with something of that abiding confidence in a solid earth which is a necessary prelude to the marshalling of digestive juices, opened the front door of his house.

IV

Mrs. Masters was standing in the sitting room awaiting him. The Doctor strode in without stopping to remove his hat or place his gloves aside, a peculiar mannerism of his upon which Mrs. Masters was wont occasionally to admonish him; for the good lady was not slow to give banter for banter when the opportunity arose, and she objected to these relics of the Doctor's earlier bohemian ways. But for the moment her mood seemed to be rather one of blandishment.

"A young lady called to see you this evening," she announced, smilingly.

The Doctor removed his hat as though in honour of the mere mention of his visitor. "Did you give her my love?" was his light rejoinder, hat still poised at an elegant angle.

"Indeed, no," retorted Mrs. Masters, "it wouldn't be my place to give such messages. Not as though she weren't inquisitive enough—with asking questions about this and that. As though it were any business of 'ers 'ow you choose to arrange your house'old."

"On the contrary, I am flattered," said the Doctor, inwardly chafing at this new example of Lilian's originality. "But tell me, Mrs. Masters, am I not becoming more successful with the ladies?" As he spoke, he flicked with his gloves the reflection of himself in the mirror.

"You don't need to be reminded of that fact, I'm sure," sighed Mrs. Masters, "life sits lightly enough on you. I fear, too lightly. If I might venture to say so, a man in your position ought to take life more seriously."

"My patients would disagree with you."

"Ah, well, I grant you that. They say you cure more with your tongue than with your physic."

"I certainly value my wit more than my prescriptions," laughingly agreed the Doctor, "But tell me, what was the lady's impression of my *ménage*? And that reminds me, you have not told me her name yet. Did she carry a red parasol, or was it a white one?"

"I'm sure I never noticed," frowned Mrs. Masters, "such things don't interest me. But her name was Miss Lilian Payne—"

The Doctor interrupted with a guffaw. "Come, Mrs. Masters, we need not beat about the bush. I rather fancy you are aware of our relationship. Did you find her agreeable?"

"Pretty middling," said Mrs. Masters, reluctantly, "although at first I was put out by her manners. Such airs these modern young women give themselves. But she got round me in the end with her pretty ways, and I found myself taking 'er all round the 'ouse, which of course I ought not to 'ave done without your permission."

"Tell me," said the Doctor, without moving a muscle in his face, "was she satisfied with her tour of my premises?"

"There now!" exclaimed Mrs. Masters, hastily arranging an antimacassar on the back of a chair, "I won't tell you that, because, of course, I don't know."

She retreated towards the door.

"But did she leave any message?" enquired the Doctor, fixing her with his eye-glass.

"Botheration!" ejaculated Mrs. Masters, in aggrieved tones, "now you've asked me and I've got to tell you. I wanted to keep it back. Oh, I do hope you're not going to be disappointed. I'm sure she didn't really mean it."

"What did she say," demanded the Doctor, irritably.

"She says to me, she says, 'Tell him there's nothing doing.'"

There was a pause. Mrs. Masters drew in her lip and folded her arms stiffly. The Doctor stared hard at her for a moment, and almost betrayed himself. Then he threw back his head and laughed with the air of a man to whom all issues of life, great and small, had become the object of a graduated hilarity. "Then upon some other lady will fall the 'supreme honour,'" he observed.

"You mean—" began Mrs. Masters, and then eyed him with the meaning expression of a woman scenting danger or happiness for some other woman. "That young lady is not suited to you, at all events," she continued, shaking her head.

"Evidently not," replied the Doctor, carelessly, "but it is not of the slightest importance. As I have said, the honour—"

"Ah," broke in Mrs. Masters, "there's only one woman for you, and you have yet to find her."

"There's only one woman for me, and that is the woman who will marry me. Nay, don't lecture me, Mrs. Masters. I perceive the admonishment leaping to your eye. I am determined to approach this question of matrimony in the spirit of levity which you admit is my good or evil genius. Life is a comedy, and in order to shine in it one must assume the *rôle* of the buffoon who rollicks through the scenes, poking fun at those sober-minded folk upon whose earnestness the very comedy depends. I will marry in jest and repent in laughter."

"Incorrigible man," said Mrs. Masters. But the Doctor had turned his back upon her, unwilling to reveal the sudden change in his features. Even as he spoke those light words, there came to him the reflection that he did not really mean them, and his pose seemed to crumble to dust. He had lived up to these nothings for years, but now he knew that they were nothings. As though to crown the irritations of a trying day, there came to him the conviction that his whole life had been an affair of studied gestures, of meticulous gesticulations.

V

Over an unsatisfactory meal he tried to think things out, conscious all the time that he was missing gastronomical opportunities through sheer inattention.

Of course, Lilian's impression of his *ménage* would have been unsatisfactory, even though he had escorted her over the house himself; but it was highly significant that she should have preferred to come alone. Holding advanced opinions about the simplification of the house, and of the woman's duties therein, she would regard his establishment as unwieldy, overcrowded, old-fashioned, even musty. It would represent to her unnecessary responsibilities, labour without reward, meaningless ostentation. The Doctor's own tastes lay in the direction of massive, ornate furniture, rich carpets and hangings, a multiplicity of ornaments. He liked a house filled to the brim with expensive things. He was a born collector and accumulator of odds and ends, of things that had become necessary to his varying moods. He was proud of his house, with its seventeen rooms, including two magnificent reception rooms, four spare bedrooms in a state of constant readiness, like fire-stations, for old friends who always said they were coming and never did; its elaborate kitchen arrangements and servants' quarters. Then there were cosy little rooms which a woman of taste would be able to decorate according to her whim, workrooms, snuggeries, halls and landings. There was much in the place that ought to appeal to a woman with right instincts.

Was Lilian going to destroy their happiness for the sake of these modern heresies? Surely she would not throw him over now; and yet her message left that impression. Nowadays women were so led by their sensibilities. Lilian's hypersensitive nature might revolt at the prospect of living with him in the surroundings of his own choice.

He would look such a fool if the match did not come off. He had made so many sacrifices for her sake, sacrifices that were undignified, but necessary in a country town where every detail of daily life speedily becomes common knowledge. That was why he would appear so ridiculous if the marriage did not take place. It had been necessary, in the first place, to establish himself in the particular clique favoured by Lilian's parents, and although this manoeuvre had involved a further lapse from his already partly disestablished principles, and an almost palpable insincerity, the Doctor had adopted it without much scruple. He had resigned his position as Vicar's churchwarden at the rather eucharistic parish church, and become a mere worshipper in a back pew at the Baptist chapel; for Lilian's father favoured the humble religion of self-made men. He had subscribed to the local temperance society, and contributed medical articles to the local paper on the harmful effects of alcohol and the training of midwives. In the winter evenings he gave lantern lectures on "The Wonders of Science." He organised a P.S.A., delivered addresses to Young Men Only, and generally did all he could to advance the Baptist cause, which, in Great Wymering, stood not only for simplicity of religious belief, but also for the simplification of daily life aided by scientific knowledge and common sense. All that had been necessary in order to become legitimately intimate with the Payne family; for they enjoyed the most aggravating good health, and the Doctor had grown tired of awaiting an opportunity to dispense anti-toxins in exchange for tea.

But the class to which the Paynes belonged were not really humble. They were urban in origin, and the semi-aristocratic tradition of Great Wymering was opposed to them. They had come down from the London suburbs in response to advertisements of factory sites, and their enterprise had been amazing. Within a few years Great Wymering had ceased to be a pleasing country town, with historic associations dating back to the first Roman occupation; it was merely known to travellers on the South-Eastern and Chatham railway as the place where Payne's Dog Biscuits were manufactured.

The Doctor, in establishing himself in the right quarter, had forgotten to allow for the fact that the force that had lifted the Paynes out of their urban obscurity had descended to their daughter, Lilian had been expensively educated, and although the Doctor denied it to himself a hundred times a week, there was no evading the fact that an acute brain slumbered behind her rather immobile beauty. True, the fruits of her learning languished a little in Great Wymering, and that beyond a slight permanent frown and a disposition to argue about modern problems, she betrayed no revolt against the narrowness of her existence, but appeared, graceful and willowy, at garden parties or whist drives. It was the development of her mind that the Doctor feared, especially as, all unconsciously at first, he had acted as its chief stimulant. During their talks together he had spoken too many a true word in jest; and his witticisms had revealed to Lilian a whole world about which to think and theorise.

He glanced up at her photograph on the mantelpiece. If there was a flaw in the composition of her fair, Saxon beauty, it was that the mouth was a little too large and opened rather too easily, disclosing teeth that were not as regular as they should be. But nature's blunder often sets the seal on man's choice, and to the Doctor this trifling fault gave warmth and vivacity to a face that might easily have been cold and impassive, especially as her eyes were steel blue and she had no great art in the use of them. Her voice, too, often startled the listener by its occasional note that suggested an excitability of temperament barely under control.

In vain the Doctor tried to throw off his heavy reflections and assume the air of gaiety usual to him when drinking his coffee and thinking of Lilian. Such an oppression could hardly be ascribed to the malady of love. It was not Romeo's "heavy lightness, serious vanity." It was a deep perplexity, a grave foreboding that something had gone hideously wrong with him, something that he was unable to diagnose. It could not be that he was growing old. As a medical man he knew his age to an artery. And yet, in spite of his physical culture and rather deliberate chastity, he felt suddenly that he was not a fit companion for this young girl with her resilient mind. He had always been fastidious about morals, without being exactly moral, but there was something within him that he did not care to contemplate. It almost seemed as though the sins of the mind were more deadly than those of the flesh, for the latter expressed themselves in action and re-action, while the former remained in the mind, there to poison and corrupt the very source of all activity.

What was it then—this feeling of a fixation of himself—of a slowing down of his faculties? Was it some strange new malady of the modern world, a state of mind as yet not crystallised by the poet or thinker? It was difficult to get a clear image to express his condition; yet that was his need. There was no phrase or word in his memory that could symbolise his feeling.

And then there was the Clockwork man—something else to think about, to be wondered at.

At this point in the Doctor's reflections the door opened suddenly and Mrs. Masters ushered in the Curate, very dishevelled and obviously in need of immediate medical attention. His collar was all awry, and the look upon his face was that of a man who has looked long and fixedly at some object utterly frightful and could not rid himself of the image. "I've had a shock," he began, trying pathetically to smile recognition. "Sorry disturb you—meal time—" He sank into a saddle-bag chair and waved limp arms expressively. "There was a man—" he got out.

The Doctor wiped his mouth and produced a stethoscope. His manner became soothingly professional. He murmured sympathetic phrases and pulled a chair closer to his patient.

"There was a man," continued the Curate, in ancient-mariner-like tones, "at the Templars' Hall. I thought he was the conjurer, but he wasn't—at least, I don't think so. He did things—impossible things—"

"What sort of things," enquired the Doctor, slowly, as he listened to the Curate's heart. "You must make an effort to steady yourself."

"*He*—he made things appear," gasped the Curate, with a great effort, "out of nowhere—positively."

"Well, isn't that what conjurers are supposed to do?" observed the Doctor, blandly.

But the Curate shook his head. Fortunately, in his professional character there was no need for the Doctor to exhibit surprise. On the contrary, it was necessary, for his patient's sake, to exercise control. He leaned against the mantelpiece and listened attentively to the Curate's hurried account of his encounter with the Clockwork man, and shook his head gravely.

"Well, now," he prescribed, "complete rest for a few days, in a sitting posture. I'll give you something to quieten you down. Evidently you've had a shock."

"It's very hard," the Curate complained, "that my infirmity should have prevented me from seeing more. The spirit was willing but the flesh was weak."

"Very likely," the Doctor suggested, "someone has played a trick upon you. Perhaps your own nerves are partly to blame. Men with highly strung nerves like you are very liable to—er—hallucinations."

"I wonder," said the Curate, grasping the edge of his chair, "I wonder, now, if Moses felt like this when he saw the burning bush."

"Ah, very likely," rejoined the Doctor, glad of the opportunity to enforce his analogy. "There's not the least doubt that many so-called miracles in the past had their origin in some pathological condition improperly understood at the time. Moses probably suffered from some sort of hysteria—a sort of hypnosis. Even in those days there was the problem of nervous breakdown."

His voice died away. The Curate was not actually shaking his head, but there was upon his features an expression of incredulity, the like of which the Doctor had not seen before upon a human face, for it was the incredulity of a man to whom all arguments against the incredible are in themselves unbelievable. It was a grotesque expression, and with it there went a pathetic fluttering of the Curate's eyelids, a twitching of his lips, a clasping of small white hands.

"I'm afraid your explanation won't hold water," he rejoined. "I can't bring myself not to believe in what I saw. You see, all my life I have been trying to believe in miracles, in manifestations. I have always said that if only we could bring ourselves to accept what is not obvious. My best sermons have been upon that subject: of the desirability of getting ourselves into the receptive state. Sometimes the Vicar has objected. He seemed to think I was piling it on deliberately. But I assure you, Doctor Allingham, that I have always wanted to believe—and, in this case, it was only my infirmity and my unfortunate nervousness that led me to lose such an opportunity."

The Doctor drew himself up stiffly, and just perceptibly indicated the door. "I think you need a holiday," he remarked, "and a change from theological pursuits. And don't forget. Rest, for a few days, in a sitting posture."

"Thank you," the Curate beamed, "I'm afraid the Vicar will be very annoyed, but it can't be helped."

They were in the hall now, and the Doctor was holding the street door open.

"But it *happened*," the Curate whispered. "It really did *happen*—and we shall hear and see more. I only hope I shall be well enough to stand it. We are living in great days."

He hovered on the doorstep, rubbing his hands together and looking timidly up at the stars as though half expecting to see a sign. "It distressed me at first," he resumed, "because he was such an odd-looking person, and the whole experience was really on the humorous side. I wanted to laugh at him, and it made me feel so disgraceful. But I'm quite sure he was a manifestation of something, perhaps an apotheosis."

"Don't hurry home," warned the Doctor. "Take things quietly."

"Oh, yes, of course. The body is a frail instrument. One forgets that. So good of you. But the spirit endures. Good night."

He glided along the deserted High Street. The Doctor held the door ajar for a long while and watched that frail figure, nursing a tremendous conviction and hurrying along, in spite of instructions to the contrary.

CHAPTER 7

The Clockwork Man Explains Himself

I

LATE THAT EVENING the Doctor returned from a confinement case, which had taken him to one of the outlying villages near Great Wymering. The engine was grinding and straining as the car slowly ascended a steep incline that led into the town; and the Doctor leaned forward in the seat, both hands gripping the wheel, and his eyes peering through the windscreen at the stretch of well-lit road ahead of him.

He had almost reached the top of the hill, and was about to change his gear, when a figure loomed up out of the darkness and made straight for the car. The Doctor hastily jammed his brake down, but too late to avert a collision. There was a violent bump ; and the next moment the car began running backwards down the hill, followed by the figure, who had apparently suffered no inconvenience from the contact.

Aware that his brakes were not strong enough to avert another disaster, the Doctor deftly turned the car sideways and ran backwards into the hedge. He leapt out into the road and approached the still moving figure.

"What the devil!"

The figure stopped with startling suddenness, but offered no explanation.

"What are you playing at?" the Doctor demanded, glancing at the crumpled bonnet of his car. "It's a wonder I didn't kill you."

And then, as he approached nearer to that impassive form, staring at him with eyes that glittered luridly in the darkness, he recognised something familiar about his appearance. At the same moment he realised that this singular individual had actually run into the car without apparently incurring the least harm. The reflection rendered the Doctor speechless for a few seconds; he could only stare confusedly at the Clockwork man. The latter remained static, as though, in his turn, trying to grasp the significance of what had happened.

It occurred to the Doctor that here was an opportunity to investigate certain matters.

"Look here," he broke out, after a collected pause, "once and for all, who are you?"

A question, sharply put, generally produced some kind of effect upon the Clockwork man. It seemed to release the mechanism in his brain that made coherent speech possible. But his reply was disconcerting.

"Who are *you*?" he demanded, after a preliminary click or two.

"I am a doctor," said Allingham, rather taken back, "a medical man. If you are hurt at all—"

An extra gleam of light shone in the other's eye, and he seemed to ponder deeply over this statement.

"Does that mean that you can mend people?" he enquired, at last.

"Why yes, I suppose it does," Allingham admitted, not knowing what else to say.

The Clockwork man sighed, a long, whistling sigh. "I wish you would mend me. I'm all wrong you know. Something has got out of place, I think. My clock won't work properly."

"Your clock," echoed the doctor.

"It's rather difficult to explain," the Clockwork man continued, "but so far as I remember, doctors were people who used to mend human beings before the days of the clock. Now they are called mechanics. But it amounts to the same thing."

"If you will come with me to my surgery," the Doctor suggested, with as much calmness as he could assume, "I'll do my best for you."

The Clockwork man bowed stiffly. "Thank you. Of course, I'm a little better than I was, but my ears still flap occasionally."

The Doctor scarcely heard this. He had turned aside and stooped down in order to rewind the engine of his car. When he looked up again he beheld an extraordinary sight.

The Clockwork man was standing by his side, a comic expression of pity and misgiving animating his crude features. With one hand he was softly stroking the damaged bonnet of the car.

"Poor thing," he was saying, "It must be suffering dreadfully. I *am* so sorry."

Allingham paused in the turning of the handle and stared, aghast, at his companion. There was no mistaking the significance of the remark, and it had been spoken in tones of strange tenderness. Rapidly there swept across the Doctor's mind a sensation of complete conviction. If there was any further proof required of the truth of Gregg's conjecture, surely it was expressed in this apparently insane and yet obviously sincere solicitude on the part of the Clockwork man for an inanimate machine? He recognised in the mechanism before him a member of his own species!

The thing was at once preposterous and rational, and the Doctor almost yielded to a desire to laugh hysterically. Then, with a final jerk of the handle, he started the engine and opened the door of the car for the Clockwork man to enter. The latter, after making several absurd attempts to mount the step in the ordinary manner, stumbled and fell head foremost into the interior. The Doctor followed, and picking up the prostrate figure, placed him in a sitting posture upon the seat. He was extraordinarily light, and there was something about the feel of his body that sent a thrill of apprehension down the Doctor's spine. He was thoroughly frightened by now, and the manner in which his companion took everything for granted only increased his alarm.

"I know one thing," the Clockwork man remarked, as the car began to move, "I'm devilish hungry."

II

That the Clockwork man was likely to prove a source of embarrassment to him in more ways than one was demonstrated to the Doctor almost as soon as they entered the house. Mrs. Masters, who was laying the supper, regarded the visitor with a slight huffiness. He obtruded upon her vision as an extra meal for which she was not prepared. And the Doctor's manner was not reassuring. He seemed, for the time being, to lack that urbanity which usually enabled him to smooth over the awkward situations in life. It was unfortunate, perhaps, that he should have allowed Mrs. Masters to develop an attitude of distrust, but he was nervous, and that was sufficient to put the good lady on her guard.

"Lay an extra place, will you, Mrs. Masters," the Doctor had requested as they entered the room.

"I'm afraid you'll 'ave to make do," was the sharp rejoinder, for there was not much on the table, and the Doctor favoured a light supper. "There's watercress," she added, defensively.

"Care for watercress?" enquired the Doctor, trying hard to glance casually at his guest.

The Clockwork man stared blankly at his interrogator. "Watercress," he remarked, "is not much in my line. Something solid, if you have it, and as much as possible. I feel a trifle faint."

He sat down rather hurriedly, on the couch, and the Doctor scanned him anxiously for symptoms. But there were none of an alarming character. He had not removed his borrowed hat and wig.

"Bring up anything you can find," the Doctor whispered in Mrs. Masters' ear, "my friend has had rather a long journey. Anything you can find. Surely we have things in tins."

His further suggestions were drowned by an enormous hyæna-like yawn coming from the direction of the couch. It was followed by another, even more prodigious. The room fairly vibrated with the Clockwork man's uncouth expression of omnivorous appetite,

"Bless us!" Mrs. Masters could not help saying. "Manners!"

"Is there anything you particularly fancy?" enquired the Doctor.

"Eggs," announced the figure on the couch. "Large quantities of eggs—infinite eggs."

"See what you can do in the matter of eggs," urged the Doctor, and Mrs. Masters departed, with the light of expedition in her eye, for to feed a hungry man, even one whom she regarded with suspicion, was part of her religion.

"I'm afraid I put you to great inconvenience," murmured the visitor, still yawning and rolling about on the couch. "The fact is, I ought to be able to *produce* things—but that part of me seems to have gone wrong again. I did make a start—but it was only a flash in the pan. So sorry if I'm a nuisance."

"Not at all," said the Doctor, endeavouring without much success to treat his guest as an ordinary being, "I am to blame. I ought to have realised that you would require nourishment. But, of course, I am still in the dark—"

He paused abruptly, aware that certain peculiar changes were taking place in the physiognomy of the Clockwork man. His strange organism seemed to be undergoing a series of exceedingly swift and complicated physical and chemical processes. His complexion changed colour rapidly, passing from its usual pallor to a deep greenish hue, and then to a hectic flush. Concurrent with this, there was a puzzling movement of the corpuscles and cells just beneath the skin.

The Doctor was scarcely as yet in the mind to study these phenomena accurately. At the back of his mind there was the thought of Mrs. Masters returning with the supper. He tried to resume ordinary speech, but the Clockwork man seemed abstracted, and the unfamiliarity of his appearance increased every second. It seemed to the Doctor that he had remembered a little dimple on the middle of the Clockwork man's chin, but now he couldn't see the dimple. It was covered with something brownish and delicate, something that was rapidly spreading until it became almost obvious.

"You see," exclaimed the Doctor, making a violent effort to ignore his own perceptions, "it's all so unexpected. I'm afraid I shan't be able to render you much assistance until I know the actual facts, and even then—"

He gripped the back of a chair. It was no longer possible for him to deceive himself about the mysterious appearance on the Clockwork man's chin. He was growing a beard—swiftly and visibly. Already some of the hairs had reached to his collar.

"I *beg* your pardon," said the Clockwork man, suddenly becoming conscious of the hirsute development. "Irregular growth—most inconvenient—it's due to my condition—I'm all to pieces, you know—things happen spontaneously." He appeared to be struggling hard to reverse some process within himself, but the beard continued to grow.

The Doctor found his voice again. "Great heavens," he burst out, in a hysterical shout. "Stop it. You *must* stop it—I simply can't stand it."

He had visions of a room full of golden brown beard. It was the most appalling thing he had ever witnessed, and there was no trickery about it. The beard had actually grown before his eyes, and it had now reached to the second button of the Clockwork man's waistcoat. And, at any moment, Mrs. Masters might return!

Suddenly, with a violent effort involving two sharp flappings of his ears, the Clockwork man mastered his difficulty. He appeared to set in action some swift depilatory process. The beard vanished as if by magic. The doctor collapsed into a chair.

"You mustn't do anything like that again," he muttered hoarsely. "You—must—let—me—know—when—you—feel it—coming on."

In spite of his agitation, it occurred to him that he must be prepared for worse shocks than this. It was no use giving way to panic. Incredible as had been the cricketing performance, the magical flight, and now this ridiculously sudden growth of beard, there were indications about the Clockwork man that pointed to still further abnormalities. The Doctor braced himself up to face the worst; he had no theory at all with which to explain these staggering manifestations, and it seemed more than likely that the ghastly serio-comic figure seated on the couch would presently offer some explanation of his own.

A few moments later Mrs. Masters entered the room bearing a tray with the promised meal. True to her instinct, the good soul must have searched the remotest corners of her pantry in order to provide what she evidently regarded as but an apology of a repast. Little did she know for what Brobdingnagian appetite she was catering! At the sight of the six gleaming white eggs in their cups, the guest made a movement expressive of the direction of his desire, if not of very sanguine hope of their fulfilment. Besides eggs, there were several piles of sandwiches, bread and butter, and assorted cakes.

Mrs. Masters had scarcely murmured her apologies for the best she could do at such short notice, and retired, than the Clockwork man set to with an avidity that appalled and disgusted the Doctor. The six eggs were cracked and swallowed in as many seconds. The rest of the food disappeared in a series of jerks, accompanied by intense vibration of the jaws;

the whole process of swallowing resembling the pulsations of the cylinders of a petrol engine. So rapid were the vibrations, that the whole of the lower part of the Clockwork man's face was only visible as a multiplicity of blurred outlines.

The commotion subsided as abruptly as it had begun, and the Doctor enquired, with as much grace as his outraged instincts would allow, whether he could offer him any more.

"I have still," said the Clockwork man, locating his feeling by placing a hand sharply against his stomach, "an emptiness here."

"Dear me," muttered the Doctor, "you find us rather short at present. I must think of something." He went on talking, as though to gain time. "It's quite obvious, of course, that you need more than an average person. I ought to have realised. There would be exaggerated metabolism—naturally, to sustain exaggerated function. But, of course, the—er—motive force behind this extraordinary efficiency of yours is still a mystery to me. Am I right in assuming that there is a sort of mechanism?"

"It makes everything go faster," observed the Clockwork man, "and more accurately."

"Quite," murmured the Doctor. He was leaning forward now, with his elbows resting on the table and his head on one side. "I can see that. There are certain things about you that strike one as being obvious. But what beats me at present is how—and where—" he looked, figuratively speaking, at the inside of the Clockwork man, "I mean, in what part of your anatomy the—er—motive force is situated."

"The functioning principle," said the Clockwork man, "is distributed throughout, but the clock—" His words ran on incoherently for a few moments and ended in an abrupt explosion that nearly lifted him out of his seat. "Beg pardon—what I mean to say is that the clock—wallabaloo—wum—wum—"

"I am prepared to take that for granted," put in the Doctor, coughing slightly.

"You must understand," resumed the Clockwork man, making a rather painful effort to fold his arms and look natural, "you must understand—

click—click—that it is difficult for me to carry on conversation in this manner. Not only are my speech centres rather disordered—G-r-r-r-r-r—but I am not really accustomed to expressing my thoughts in this way (here there was a loud spinning noise, like a sewing machine, and rising to a rapid crescendo). My brain is—so—constituted that action—except in a multiform world—is bound to be somewhat spasmodic—Pfft—Pfft—Pfft. In fact—Pfft—it is only—Pfft—because I am in such a hope—hope—hopeless condition that I am able to converse with you at all."

"I see," said Allingham, slowly, "it is because you are, so to speak, temporarily incapacitated, that you are able to come down to the level of our world."

"It's an extra—ordinary world," exclaimed the other, with a sudden vehemence that seemed to bring about a spasm of coherency.

"I can't get used to it. Everything is so elementary and restricted. I wouldn't have thought it possible that even in the twentieth century things would have been so backward. I always thought that this age was supposed to be the beginning. History says the nineteenth and twentieth centuries were full of stir and enquiry. The mind of man was awakening. But it is strange how little has been done. I see no signs of the great movement. Why, you have not yet grasped the importance of the machines."

"We have automobiles and flying machines," interrupted Allingham, weakly.

"And you treat them like slaves," retorted the Clockwork man. "That fact was revealed to me by your callous behaviour towards your motor car. It was not until man began to respect the machines that his real history begun. What ideas have you about the relation of man to the outer cosmos?"

"We have a theory of relativity," Allingham ventured.

"Einstein!" The Clockwork man's features altered just perceptibly to an expression of faint surprise. "Is he already born?"

"He is beginning to be understood. And some attempt is being made to popularise his theory. But I don't know that I altogether agree."

The Doctor hesitated, aware of the uselessness of dissension upon such a subject where his companion was concerned. Another idea came into his head. "What sort of a world is yours? To look at, I mean. How does it appear to the eye and touch?"

"It is a *multiform* world," replied the Clockwork man (he had managed to fold his arms now, and apart from a certain stiffness his attitude was fairly normal). "Now, your world has a certain definite shape. That is what puzzles me so. There is one of everything. One sky, and one floor. Everything is fixed and stable. At least, so it appears to me. And then you have objects placed about in certain positions, trees, houses, *lamp-posts*—and they never alter their positions. It reminds me of the scenery they used in the old theatres. Now, in my world everything is constantly moving, and there is not one of everything, but always there are a great many of each thing. The universe has no definite shape at all. The sky does not look, like yours does, simply a sort of inverted bowl. It is a shapeless void. But what strikes me so forcibly about your world is that everything appears to be leading somewhere, and you expect always to come to the end of things. But in my world everything goes on for ever."

"But the streets and houses?" hazarded Allingham, "aren't they like ours?"

The Clockwork man shook his head. "We have houses, but they are not full of things like yours are, and we don't *live* in them. They are simply places where we go when we take ourselves to pieces or overhaul ourselves. They are—" his mouth opened very wide, "the nearest approach to fixed objects that we have, and we regard them as jumping-off places for successive excursions into various dimensions. Streets are of course unnecessary, since the only object of a street is to lead from one place to another, and we do that sort of thing in other ways. Again, our houses are not placed together in the absurd fashion of yours. They are anywhere and everywhere, and nowhere and nowhen. For instance, I live in the day before yesterday and my friend in the day after to-morrow."

"I begin to grasp what you mean," said Allingham, digging his chin into his hands, "as an idea, that is. It seems to me that, to borrow the words of Shakespeare, I have long dreamed of such a kind of man as you. But now that you are before me, in the—er—flesh, I find myself unable to accept you."

The unfortunate Doctor was trying hard to substitute a genuine interest in the Clockwork man for a feeling of panic, but he was not very successful. "You seem to me," he added, rather lamely, "so very theoretical."

And then he remembered the sudden growth of beard, and decided that it was useless to pursue that last thin thread of suspicion in his mind. For several seconds he said nothing at all, and the Clockwork man seemed to take advantage of the pause in order to wind himself up to a new pitch of coherency.

"It would be ridiculous," he began, after several thoracic bifurcations, "for me to explain myself more fully to you. Unless you had a clock you couldn't possibly understand. But I hope I have made it clear that my world is a multiform world. It has a thousand manifestations as compared to one of yours. It is a world of many dimensions, and every dimension is crowded with people and things. Only they don't get in each other's way, like you do, because there are always other dimensions at hand."

"That I can follow," said the Doctor, wrinkling his brows, "that seems to me fairly clear. I can just grasp that, as the hypothesis of another sort of world. But what I don't understand, what I can't begin to understand, is how you work, how this mechanism which you talk about functions."

He delivered this last sentence rather in the manner of an ultimatum, and the Clockwork man seemed to brood over it for a few seconds He was apparently puzzled by the question, and hard mechanical lines appeared upon his forehead and began slowly chasing one another out of existence. It reminded the Doctor of Venetian blinds being pulled up and down very rapidly.

"Well," the reply was shot out at last, "how do *you* work?" The repartee of the Clockwork man was none the less effective for being suspended, as it were, for a second or two before delivery.

The doctor gasped slightly and released his hold upon a mustard pot. He came up to the rebound with a new suggestion. "Now, that's a good idea. We might arrive at something by comparison. I never thought of that." He grasped the mustard pot again and tried to arrange certain matters in his mind. "It's a little difficult to know where to begin," he temporised.

"Begin at the end, if you like," suggested the Clockwork man, affably. "It's all the same to me. First and last, upside or inside, front or back—it all conveys the same idea to me."

"We are creatures of action," hazarded the Doctor, with the air of a man embarking upon a long mental voyage, "we act from certain motives. There is a principle known as Cause and Effect. Everything is related. Every action has its equal and opposite reaction. Nobody can do anything, or even think anything, without producing some change, however slight, in the general flow of things. Every movement that we make, almost every thought that passes through our minds, starts another ripple upon the surface of time, upon this endless stream of cause and effect."

"Ah," interrupted the Clockwork man, placing a finger to the side of his nose, "I begin to understand. You work upon a different principle, or rather an antiquated principle. You see, all that has been solved now. The clock works all that out in advance. It calculates ahead of our conscious selves. No doubt we still go through the same processes, *sub-consciously*, all such processes that relate to Cause and Effect. But we, that is, ourselves, are the resultant of such calculations, and the only actions we are conscious of are those which are expressed as *consequents*."

Allingham passed a hand across his forehead. "It all seems so feasible," he remarked, "once you grasp the mechanism. But what I don't understand—"

Here, however, the discussion came to an abrupt conclusion, for something was happening to the Clockwork man.

CHAPTER 8
The Clock

I

AT FIRST IT SEEMED to the Doctor that his companion was about to explain matters further. There was still something vaguely communicative about his manner, and a kind of noise issued from his rapidly moving jaws.

But it was not a human noise. It began with a succession of deep-toned growls and grunts, and ended abruptly in a distinct bark.

"Hydrophobia," flashed through the Doctor's mind, but he dismissed the idea immediately. He had lit a cigarette in order to soothe his nerves. He was trying so hard to rationalise the whole proceeding, to fit the Clock-work man into some remotely possible order of things; but it was a difficult process, for no sooner had he grouped certain ideas in his head than some fresh manifestation took place which rendered all previous theories futile. At the present moment, for instance, it was obvious that some new kind of structural alteration was taking place in the Clockwork man's physiognomy. The phenomenon could hardly be classed in the same category as the sudden growth of beard, although there were points in common. Hair was again visible, this time spread all over the rounded face and on the jaw; the nose was receding and flattening out; the eyes were dwindling in size, and the expression in them changed into a dull stare. The bark was repeated and followed by an angry rumbling.

The Doctor dropped his cigarette on the plate before him and grasped the edges of the table. His eyes were riveted upon that ghastly spectacle of transmutation.

"Oh, God," he cried out, at last, and shivering from head to foot. "Are you doing these things on purpose to frighten me, or can't you, *can't* you help it? Do you think I don't believe you? Do you think I can keep on deceiving myself? I tell you I'm ready to believe anything—I capitulate—I only ask you to let me down lightly. I'm only human, and human nerves weren't made to stand this."

"G-R-R-R-r-r-r-r," growled the Clockwork man. "WOW—WOW—can't help it—WOUGH—WOUGH—most regrettable—wow—wow—atavism—tendency to return—remote species—moment's notice—family failing—*Darwinism*—better in a moment—something gone wrong with the controls. *There—that's done it.* Phew!"

His face suddenly cleared, and all trace of the canine resemblance vanished as if by magic. He got up and took two or three jerk-like strides up and down the room. "Must keep going—when I feel like this—either food or violent stimulus—otherwise the confounded thing runs down—and there you are."

He paused and confronted Allingham, who had risen from his chair and was still trembling.

"How can I help it?" implored the Clockwork man, in despair. "They made me like this. I don't want to alarm you—but, you know, it alarms *me* sometimes. You can't imagine how trying it is to feel that at any moment you might change into something else—some horrible tree-climbing ancestor. The thing ought not to happen, but it's always possible. They should have thought of that when they made the clock."

"It mustn't happen," said the Doctor, recovering slightly, "that's the flat fact. If it's food you require, then food you shall have."

It had suddenly flashed across his fevered mind that downstairs in the surgery there lay a collection of tinned foods and patent medicines, samples that had been sent for him to test. Rather than risk a further manifestation of collapse on the part of the Clockwork-man, he would sacrifice these.

II

He was only just in time. On the way down the stairs that led to the basement surgery the Clockwork man began to flap his ears violently, and it was then that the Doctor noticed for the first time this circumstance that had so puzzled Arthur Withers. But the faculty seemed, in comparison with other exhibitions, a mere trifle, a sort of mannerism that one might expect from a being so strangely constituted.

Pushing his companion into the surgery, the Doctor commenced opening tins for all he was worth. The process calmed him, and he had time to think a little. For half an hour he opened tins, and passed them over to the Clockwork man, without noticing very much what the latter did with them. Then he went on to bottles containing patent foods, phosphates, hypophosphates, glycero-hypophosphates, all the phosphates in fact, combined with malt or other substances, which might be considered almost necessary as an auxiliary diet for the Clockwork man.

At least, the latter seemed grateful to receive whatever was given to him, and his general manner became decidedly more possible. There seemed less chance now of a drastic relapse. The Doctor had locked the door of the surgery. It would be embarrassing to be discovered in such circumstances, and Mrs. Masters might faint with horror at the sight of the empty tins and bottles and the gorging visitor. It was symptomatic of the Doctor's frame of mind that even now the one thing he dreaded more than anything else was the intrusion of a curious world into this monstrous proceeding. He had been forced into accepting the evidence of his own eyes, but there still remained in him a strong desire to hush up the affair, to protect the world at large from so fierce a shock to its established ideas.

The surgery was a low-pitched apartment, and it was approached by patients from the outside by way of the area steps. One door communicated with the dark passage that led to the kitchen quarters, and the other opened directly upon the area. A double row of shelves, well stocked with bottles, occupied the centre of the room and divided it into two halves. Beneath the window stood the Doctor's neat bureau, and to the left of this was a low couch beside the wall. A shaded lamp on the desk was sufficient to light the room for ordinary purposes; but there was a gas burner near the further door, which had to be lit when the Doctor was engaged upon some very close examination or had to perform a slight operation. Directly underneath this burner there stood an arm-chair of ample proportions, and it was here that the Clockwork man had seated himself at the beginning of his orgy.

The Doctor sat upon the couch, with his hands limply hanging between his knees. He was conscious of perspiration, but made no attempt to wipe his forehead. His heart was knocking hard against his ribs, and occasionally missing a beat. He noticed this fact also, but it caused him little concern. Now and again he looked swiftly at the Clockwork man and studied his extraordinary method of mastication, the rapid vibratory movement of the jaws, the apparent absence of any kind of voluntary effort.

Uppermost in the Doctor's mind was the reflection that he of all persons should have been selected by an undiscriminating providence to undergo this distressing and entirely unprecedented experience. It was an ironic commentary upon his reactionary views and his comfortable doctrine of common sense. He had been convinced in spite of himself, and the effort to resist conviction had strained his mental powers uncomfortably. He felt very strongly his inability to cope with the many problems that would be sure to arise in connection with the Clockwork man. It was too much for one man's brain. There would have to be a convocation of all the cleverest men in Europe in order to investigate such an appalling revelation. He pictured himself in the act of introducing this genuine being from a future age, and the description he would have to give of all that had happened in connection with him. Even that prospect set his brain reeling. He would like to be able to shirk the issue. It was enough to have looked upon this archetype of the future; the problem now was to forget his existence.

But that would be impossible. The Clockwork man was the realisation of the future. There was no evading that. The future. Man had evolved into this. He had succeeded somehow in adding to his normal powers some kind of mechanism that opened up vast possibilities of action in all sorts of dimensions. There must have been an enormous preparatory period before the thing became finally possible, generations of striving and failure and further experiment. But the indefatigable spirit of man had triumphed in the end. He had arisen at last superior to Time and Space, and taken his place in the centre of the universe. It was a fulfilment of all the prophecies of the great scientists since the discovery of evolution.

Such reflections flitted hazily through the Doctor's mind as he strove in vain to find a practical solution of the problem. What was the clock?

He knew, from hearsay, that it was situated at the back of this strange being's head. Tom Driver had seen it, and described it in his clumsy fashion. Since that episode the Doctor had visualised something in the nature of an instrument affixed to the Clockwork man's head, and perhaps connected with his cerebral processes. Was it a kind of super-brain? Had there been found some means of lengthening the convolutions of the human brain, so that man's thought travelled further and so enabled him to arrive more swiftly at ultimate conclusions? That seemed suggestive. It must be that in some way the cerebral energy of man had been stored up, as electricity in a battery, and then released by mechanical processes.

At least, that was the vague conclusion that came into the Doctor's mind and stuck there. It was the only theory at all consonant with his own knowledge of human anatomy. All physiological action could be traced to the passage of nervous energy from one centre to another, and it was obvious that, in the case of the Clockwork man, such energy was subjected to enormous acceleration and probably distributed along specially prepared paths. There was nothing in the science of neuropathy to account for such disturbances and reactions. There were neural freaks—the Doctor had himself treated some remarkable cases of nervous disorder—but the behaviour of the Clockwork man could not be explained by any principle within human knowledge. Not the least puzzling circumstance about him was the fact that now and again his speech and manner made it impossible to accept the supposition of mechanical origin; whilst at other times his antics induced a positive conviction that he was really a sort of highly perfected toy.

Presently the Clockwork man got up and began walking up and down the room, in his slow, flat-footed manner.

"How do you feel now?" ventured the Doctor, arousing himself with an effort.

"Oh, so, so," sighed the other, "only so, so—I can't expect to feel myself, you know." He reached to the end of the room, and jerking himself round, started on the return journey. The Doctor arose slowly and remained standing. There was barely room for two people to walk up and down.

"Anything might happen," the Clockwork man continued, plaintively, "I feel as though I might slip again, you know—slip back another thousand years or so." He turned again. "I've got to get worse before I get better," he sighed, and then stopped to examine the rows of bottles arranged along the shelves.

"What are these?" he enquired.

"Medicines," said the Doctor, without enthusiasm.

"Do they help people to work ?"

"H'm, yes—chemical action—tonics. People get run down, and I have to give them something to stimulate the system."

"I see," the Clockwork man nodded sagely. "But they wouldn't be any use to me. What I need is adjustment, regulation." He looked hard at the doctor, with a pathetic expression of enquiry. "My clock—" he began, and stopped abruptly.

They were facing one another now. The doctor swallowed hard several times, and he felt the blood tingling in his temples. The dreaded moment had come. He had got to see this strange instrument that distinguished the Clockwork man from ordinary mortals. There was no shrinking from the eerie experience. Underneath that borrowed hat and wig there was something—something utterly strange and outside the pale of human ingenuity. In the name of common humanity it was incumbent upon the Doctor to face the shock of this revelation, and yet he shrunk from it like a frightened child. He felt no trace of curiosity, no feverish anxiety to investigate this mystery of the future. His knees trembled violently. He did not want to see the clock. He would have given a hundred pounds to be spared the ordeal before him.

Slowly, with his customary stiffness of movement, the Clockwork man raised his arms upwards and removed the soft clerical hat. He held it aloft, as though uncertain what to do with it, and the Doctor took it from him with a shaking hand.

Next moment the wig came off, and there was disclosed to the Doctor's gaze a bald cranium.

Then the Clockwork man turned himself slowly round.

The Doctor shot out a hand and gripped the framework of the shelves. As his eyes rested upon the object that now confronted him, he swung slowly round until his body was partly supported by the shelves. His mouth opened wide and remained stretched to its limit.

At first, what he saw looked like another face, only it was round and polished. A second glance made it quite plain that instead of a back to the Clockwork man's head, there was a sort of glass dial, beneath which the doctor dimly made out myriads of indicators, tiny hands that moved round a circle marked with inconceivably minute divisions. Some of the hands moved slowly, some only just visibly, whilst others spun round with such speed that they left only a blurred impression of a vibratant rotary movement. Besides the hands there were stops, queer-shaped knobs and diminutive buttons, each one marked with a small, neat number. Little metal flaps fluttered quickly and irregularly, like the indicators on a telephone switchboard. There was a faint throbbing and commotion, a suggestion of power at high pressure.

Just for a moment the Doctor tried to realise that he was looking upon the supreme marvel of human ingenuity. He made an effort to stretch his brain once more in order to grasp the significance of this paragon of eight thousand years hence. But he did not succeed. The strain of the past hour reached its first climax. He began to tremble violently. His elbow went back with a sharp jerk and smashed three bottles standing on the shelf behind him. He made little whimpering noises in his throat.

"Oh, God," he whispered, hoarsely, and then again, as though to comfort himself, "Oh, God."

III

"If you open the lid," explained the Clockwork man (and at the sound of that human voice the doctor jumped violently), "you will see certain stops, marked with numbers."

Obedient, in spite of himself, the Doctor discovered a minute hinge and swung open the glass lid. The palpitating clock, with its stir of noises slightly accentuated, lay exposed to his touch.

"Stop XI," continued the Clockwork man, in tones of sharp instruction. "Press hard. Then wind Y4 three times."

Slowly, with a wildly beating heart, the Doctor inserted a trembling finger among the interstices of those multitudinous stops and hands, and as slowly withdrew it again. He could not do this thing. For one thing, his finger was too large. It was a ridiculously clumsy instrument for so fine a purpose. What if he failed? Pressed a knob too hard or set a hand spinning in the wrong direction? The least blunder—

"I can't do it," he gasped, "I can't really. You must—excuse me."

"Be quick," said the Clockwork man, in a squeaky undertone, "something is going to happen."

So it came about that the Doctor's final action was hurried and ill-considered. It seemed to him that he must have committed some kind of assault upon the mechanism. Actually, he succeeded in pressing the knob marked XI, and the immediate result was a sort of muffled ringing sound arising from somewhere in the depths of the Clockwork man's organism.

"Registered," exclaimed the latter, triumphantly. "Now, the hand."

The Doctor found the hand and tried to twist it very slowly and carefully. He had expected the thin piece of metal to resist his touch; but it swung round with a fatal facility—five and a half times!

The Clockwork man suddenly turned round. Immediately afterwards the Doctor became aware of a series of loud popping noises, accompanied by the sound of tearing and rending. Simultaneously, some hard object hit him just over the eye, and the walls and ceiling of the little room were struck sharply by something violently expelled. And then he felt himself being pushed gently away by some pressure that was steadily insisting upon more space.

It was an effect in startling disproportion to the cause. Or, at least, so it seemed to the Doctor, who was, of course, totally ignorant about the mechanism with which he was experimenting.

"Reverse!" exclaimed the Clockwork man, in thick, suety tones. "Reverse."

Already he was several times stouter than his original self. He had burst all his buttons—which accounted for the sudden explosions—and his clothes were split all the way down, back and front. Great pouches and three new chins appeared upon his face, and lower down there was visible an enormous stomach.

The Doctor seized hold of the other's collar and turned the huge body round. His hand fumbled wildly among the stops.

"Which one?" he gasped, his face livid with fright. "Tell me what to do. In heaven's name, do you expect me to *know*?"

"Z5," came the faint rejoinder, "and reverse Y4—most important—reverse Y4."

It followed upon this experiment that the Clockwork man presently emitted a faint, quavering protest. He had certainly dwindled in bulk. His clothes hung upon him, and there was a distressing feebleness of frame. Slowly it dawned upon the Doctor that the face peering up at him was that of a very old and decrepit individual. Painful lines crossed his forehead, and there were rheumy lodgements in the corner of each eye. The change was rapidly progressive.

By this time the Doctor's condition of hysteria had given way to a sort of desperate recklessness. He had somehow to restore the Clockwork man to some semblance of passable humanity. He pressed stops and twisted hands with an entire disregard for the occasional instructions bellowed at him by the unfortunate object of his random experiments. He felt that the very worst could scarcely surpass what had already taken place. And it was obvious that the Clockwork man had but the haziest notions about his own mechanism. Evidently he was intended to be adjusted by some other person. He was not, in that sense, autonomous.

It was also manifest that the Clockwork man was capable of almost limitless adaptability. Several of the stops produced only slight changes or the first beginnings of some fundamental alteration of structure. Usually these changes were of a sufficiently alarming character to cause the Doctor immediately to check them by further experiments. The Clockwork man seemed to be an epitome of everything that had ever existed. After one experiment he developed gills. Another produced frightful atavistic snortings. There was one short-lived episode of a tail.

By the end of another five minutes the Doctor had sacrificed all scruple. His fingers played over that human keyboard with a recklessness that was born of sheer horror of his own actions. He almost fancied that he might suddenly arrive at some kind of mastery of the stunning instrument. He alternated between that delusion and trusting blindly to chance. It was indeed by accident that he discovered and pressed hard home a large stop marked simply O.

The next second he found himself contemplating what was apparently an empty heap of clothes lying upon the floor at his feet.

The Clockwork man had vanished !

"*Ah!*" screamed the Doctor, dancing round the room, and forgetting even God in his agony. "What have I done? What have I *done*?"

He knelt down and searched hastily among the clothes. There was a lump moving about very slightly, in the region of the waistcoat, a lump that was strangely soft to the touch. Then he felt the hard surface of the clock. Before he could remove the mass of clothing there broke upon the stillness a strange little cry, to the Doctor curiously familiar. It was the wail of an infant, long-drawn and pitiful.

When the Doctor found him, he appeared to be about six weeks old, and rapidly growing smaller and smaller.

Only the promptest and most fortuitous action upon the Doctor's part averted something inconceivably disastrous.

CHAPTER 9
Gregg

I

AN HOUR LATER the Doctor alone paced the floor of the little surgery.

He had done everything possible to calm himself. He had taken bromide; he had been out for a smart turn around the roads; he had forced himself to sit down and answer some letters. But it was impossible to ease the pressure of his thoughts; he felt that his brain would never cease from working round and round in a circle of hopeless enquiry. In the end, and late as it was, he had telephoned for Gregg.

The Clockwork man lay in the coal cellar, which was situated in the area, just opposite the surgery door. He lay there, stiff and stark, with an immobile expression upon his features, and his eyes and mouth wide open.

After that final collapse, the Doctor had succeeded somehow in restoring him to his normal shape; and then, by miraculous chance, he discovered a hand that, when turned, had the effect of producing in the Clockwork man an appearance of complete quiescence. He looked now more like a tailor's dummy than anything else; and the apparent absence of blood circulation and even respiration rendered the illusion almost perfect. He looked life-like without seeming to be alive.

But he was alive. The Doctor had made sure of that by certain tentative experiments; and he had also taken advantage of his passive condition in order to make a thorough examination—so far as was possible—of this marvel of the future. As a result of his investigation, the Doctor had failed to come to any definite conclusion; there was merely deepened in him a sense of outrage and revolt. It was impossible to accept the Clockwork man as a human being.

He was a tissue of physiological lies.

It could be proved beyond a shadow of doubt, and by reference to all known laws of anatomy, that he did not exist.

His internal organs, heard in action through a stethoscope, resembled the noise made by the humming of a dynamo at full pitch.

And yet this wildly incredible being, this unspeakable travesty of all living organisms, this thing most opposite to humanity, actually breathed and conversed. He was a sentient being. He was more than man, for he could be turned into something else by simply pressing a stop. Properly understood, there was no doubt that the mechanism permitted the owner of it to run up and down the evolutionary scale of species according to adjustment.

There were one or two other details which the Doctor had not failed to observe.

The Clockwork man had no apparent sex.

His body was scarred and disfigured, as though many surgical operations had been performed upon it.

There was some organ faintly approximating to the human heart, but it was infinitely more powerful, and the valvular action was exceedingly complex.

Fitted into the clock, in such a way that they could be removed, were a series of long tubes with valve-like endings. The Doctor had removed one or two of these and examined them very closely, but he could not arrive at any idea of their purpose.

At every point in his examination the Doctor had found himself confronted by an elaboration, in some cases a flat contradiction, of ordinary human functions. He could not grasp even the elementary premises of a state of affairs that had made the Clockwork man possible.

II

Shortly after midnight the Doctor's expectant ear caught the sound of someone alighting from a bicycle. A moment later footsteps clattered down the area stairs, and Gregg, still attired in his cricket flannels, appeared at the open door. The smile faded from his lips as he beheld the drawn, agitated features of the Doctor.

"Hulloa," he exclaimed, "you look pretty bent."

The Doctor shut the door carefully and lifted a warning finger. "Gregg, this thing must never be known. It must never go beyond ourselves."

"Why not?" Gregg sat down on the couch and twisted his hat idly between his fingers.

"Because," said the Doctor, trying hard to control the twitching of his features, "it's too terrible. What I have seen to-night is not fit for mortal eye to behold. It's inhuman. It's monstrous !"

He sank into a chair and covered his face with his hands. The presence of another person brought a kind of relief to his pent-up feelings. He let himself go.

"Oh, God, it's the end of all things, Gregg. It's the end of all sane hopes for the human race. If it is true that in the future man *has* come to this, then the whole of history is a farce and mockery. The universe is no more than a box of conjuring tricks, and man is simply a performing monkey. I tell you, Gregg, this discovery, if it is made known, will blast everything good in existence."

"Stop a minute," exclaimed Gregg, arising in sheer astonishment, "you seem to be upset. I don't understand what you are raving about."

The Doctor stabbed a finger wildly in the direction of the coal cellar. "If you had seen what I have seen to-night, you would understand. You would be feeling exactly as I am now."

Gregg placed a hand soothingly upon his friend's shoulder. "Why didn't you send for me before? You're over-strung. This experience has been too much for you."

"I grant you that," said the Doctor, hollowly, "I know only too well what effect this shock will have upon me. You are a younger man than I am, Gregg. I am glad you have been spared this sight."

"But where is the Clockwork man?" demanded Gregg, presently.

The Doctor's finger again indicated the coal cellar. "He—he's in there—I—I managed to stop him. He—he's in a kind of sleep."

And then, as Gregg took a leisurely stride towards the door, as though to investigate matters on his own, the Doctor caught hold of his sleeve. "Don't do that. Listen, first, to what I have to tell you. I rather fancy it will take the edge off your curiosity."

Gregg swung round and sat on the couch. He lit a cigarette. He made no effort to conceal his sense of superior self-possession. The doctor took the cigarette that was preferred to him, and leaning forward tried to take a light from his companion. But his hand shook so violently that he could not manage the simple operation. In the end Gregg lit another match and held it with a steady hand.

As the Doctor told the story of what had taken place so recently in the little room, Gregg sat nursing an uplifted knee between his hands and with the cigarette drooping idly from his lips. Once or twice he interrupted with a gesture, but if he experienced astonishment he never betrayed the fact. Even the description of the sudden growth of beard did not disturb the look of calm enquiry upon his hard-set features. He seemed to be following something in his mind that elucidated the facts as they came out; and as the narrative drew to a close he nodded his head very slightly, as though having found corroboration for these strange events in some theory of his own, and *vice versa*. When at last the Doctor reached the climax of his tale there was no horror written upon Gregg's countenance. He remained impassive, a sort of buffer against which the Doctor's hysterical phrases recoiled in vain.

There was a moment's silence. The Doctor had been talking so rapidly, and he had been so swayed by his feelings, that he had scarcely noticed the other's demeanour. When he looked up Gregg was walking with a measured tread up and down the floor. He had dropped his cigarette, and his mouth was formed in the act of whistling. The Doctor started to his feet.

"What! You believe it then? You, who have not seen this mystery—you believe it?"

"Why not?" Gregg paused in his walk and looked genuinely surprised.

"But—surely!" The Doctor sat down again and groaned. "Surely you cannot accept such a story without a sign of incredulity? What state of mind is that which can believe such things without having seen them? Why, you credulous fool, I might have invented the whole thing!"

Gregg smiled. "I am one of those who are prepared to accept the miraculous at second-hand. Besides, you forget that I have already witnessed some of the Clockwork man's manifestations of ingenuity. Nothing that you have told me causes me more astonishment than I experienced on the first occasion we had reason to believe the Clockwork man was—what he is. It is all, to my mind, quite natural and logical."

"But you must admit," interpolated the Doctor, "that I might be deceiving you. I could easily do it, just to prove you in the wrong. I can assure you that nothing would suit my humour better at the present moment! Instead of which it is I who appear the fool. I never wanted to believe in the Clockwork man. I was angry with you for believing in him. Admit that it would be a just revenge on my part to hoax you."

Gregg shook his head. "You might try to do such a thing, but you would certainly fail. Besides, I know you are telling the truth. Your manner plainly shows it."

He sat down on the couch again. "Perhaps it is just as well that I did believe in the Clockwork man from the first; for while you have been going through these unpleasant experiences I have been thinking very hard, and have actually arrived at certain conclusions which are, I venture to think, amply confirmed by your story. That is why I have shown no surprise at your statements. The Clockwork man is indeed true to his type as I have imagined him; he is the very embodiment of the future as I have long envisaged it."

At these words the Doctor threw up his arms in despair. "Then I write myself down a fool," he exclaimed, "I had no such wild hope, or such equally wild despair, with regard to the future of the human race. I admit that I have been behindhand. These matters have slipped from my grasp. The calls of ordinary life have claimed me, as they must every man past his first youth. But I am ready to believe anything that can be explained."

"It is precisely because the Clockwork man can be explained," interrupted Gregg, with some eagerness, "that I find it easy to believe him."

"But how can you explain him?" protested the Doctor, with some trace of his old irritation. "You have not even seen the clock."

"Your description of it is quite good enough for me," rejoined the other, with emphasis, "I can see it in my mind's eye. Moreover, it was obvious to me, from the first, that there must exist some such instrument in order that the Clockwork man might be adjusted when necessary. One deduced that."

The Doctor shuddered slightly, and leaned his head upon his arm. "Consider yourself lucky that you never did see the clock, and that you never had the opportunity of testing its efficiency. It is all very well for you to wax enthusiastic over your theories, but facts are hard masters."

"Precisely," said Gregg, who was beginning to grow impatient with the other's manner, "and since the facts have revealed themselves, what is the use of trying to evade them? Here we have a clockwork man, a creature entirely without precedent, for there is no record of his having existed in the past, and so far as we know there has been no successful attempt to create such a being in our own times. Everything favours my original hypothesis; that he has in some way, and probably through some fault in the mechanism that controls him, lapsed into these earlier years of human existence. That seems to me feasible. If man has indeed conquered time and space, then the slightest irregularity in this new functioning principle would result in a catastrophe such as we must suppose has happened to the Clockwork man. It is more than probable that a slight adjustment would result in his speedy return to conditions more proper to his true state."

"But this does not explain him," broke in the Doctor, bitterly.

"Wait, I am coming to that. We have to get the facts firmly in our heads. First of all, there is a mechanism, a functioning principle, which causes certain processes to take place, and enables the Clockwork man to behave as no ordinary human being ever could behave. What that functioning principle is we do not yet know; we can only posit its existence—we must do that—and draw what inference we can from its results. Now, the effect of the functioning principle is clear to me, if the cause is hidden. Obviously, the effect of the mechanism is to accelerate certain processes in the purely human part of the Clockwork man's organism to such an extent that what would take years, or even generations, to take place in ordinary mortals, takes place instantaneously. Witness the growth of beard, the changes in appearance, the total collapse. Obviously, these physiological variations occur in the case of the Clockwork man very rapidly; and by adjustment any change may be produced. The problem of his normal existence hangs upon the very careful regulation of the clock, which, I take it, is the keyboard of the functioning principle. But what concerns us at present is the fact that this power of rapid growth makes the Clockwork man able to act in complete defiance of our accepted laws relating to cause and effect."

"We had an argument about that," said the Doctor, dismally. "He tried to explain that to me, but I must say he was no more successful than you are. The whole thing is a complete haze."

But Gregg took little notice of the interruption. "Once you have grasped this idea of a new sort of relativity," he continued, "once you have realised that the Clockwork man behaves in accordance with laws quite different to our own, you can proceed to find some basis for such a phenomenon. The Clockwork man behaves in a certain manner; therefore there must be some cause, however improbable it may appear to us, to account for such behaviour. Now, what is the cause of ordinary human action? It is something equally unaccountable. We can explain it in terms of a system, of a series of processes, but we do not really know what is the secret spring upon which the human animal moves. We can describe the machinery of the human body, but we do not really know what life is, or what is the real nature of the force that produces our actions. So far we know as much about the Clockwork man as we do about ourselves. The difference is confined to processes."

"All this is obvious," said the Doctor, "I have seen enough to convince me of that."

"Precisely. And because you have seen more than I have you are less able to understand the matter than I am. You cannot see the wood for the trees. Again, you were frightened out of your life. Your scientific instincts were stampeded. You saw only a hideous malformation, a neural freak, a preposterous human machine. It was inconceivable that you should have been able to think clearly under the circumstances. Consider the matter in the sober aftermath of reason, and you must agree with me that it is really not more extraordinary that a man should function by mechanical means than that he should function at all."

"I don't agree," retorted the Doctor, with unexpected sharpness. "I think it is far more amazing that a human being should function as he does, than that he should be made to function differently by mechanical means. The Clockwork man is no more wonderful, in that sense, than you or I. He is simply different—damnably different."

Gregg laughed softly. "Well, that is only another way of saying what I have already said. You seem to regard the Clockwork man as a sort of offence; he upsets your sense of decency. To me he is profoundly interesting. I accept him, and all that his curious constitution implies. Think of the triumph for the human brain. For man, thanks to this stupendous invention of the clock, has actually enlarged the universe."

"A multiform world," murmured the Doctor, recollecting the Clockwork man's description, "a world of many dimensions."

"Yes," echoed Gregg enthusiastically, "a multiform world. A world in which man moves as he will, grows as he will, behaves in every way exactly as he wills. A world set free! Think of what it means!"

"Stop," cried the Doctor, and there was almost anger in his features as he leapt to his feet. "It is you who are raving now. How can there exist such a world? And what plight has overtaken the human race, that it is now dependent upon mechanical contrivance for its actions! But, no. I refuse to believe that the Clockwork man represents the final destiny of man. He is a myth, a caricature, at the most a sort of experiment. This multiform world of which he talks so glibly is an extravagant boast. Besides, who would care to live in such a world, and with every action conditioned by an exact mechanism? Your optimism about this extraordinary affair amazes me even more than the thing itself. At the best what it means is that man has come to final ruin, not that he has achieved any real mastery of life. If all the creatures in the world eight thousand years hence are indeed clockwork men, then it is because some monstrous tyranny has come to birth in the race of man; it is because some diabolical plan has been evolved to make all men slaves. The clock may make man independent of time and space, but it obviously condemns him to an eternity of slavery. That is why I am still loath to believe in the evidence of my own eyes. That is why any explanation of this phenomenon is better than the obvious one!"

"But the proof," interjected Gregg, "you cannot escape from the facts. There lies the Clockwork man. Explain him otherwise if you can."

"I cannot," groaned the Doctor, his face hidden between his hands. And then he looked up quickly, and his eyes cleared. "Perhaps, after all, that is the consoling feature of the affair. If the Clockwork man were really capable of explanation, then indeed there would be an end to all sanity. But since he is inexplicable, there still remains the chance that we may be able to put all thought of him out of our minds. I tell you, Gregg, I can live this down, I can forget this night of horror; but not if there is an explanation to fit the case. Not if I can satisfy my reason!"

"As I remarked before," Gregg resumed, coolly, "you were not in a fit state to carry out the investigation. You could not bring yourself to accept even the obvious. Fortunately you remembered some of the most salient facts. Those tubes fitted into the clock, for example; I regard those as highly suggestive. Think of it, Allingham! The energy of generations compressed into a tube and so utilised by a single individual. For that is what must have happened in the year 8000. The scientists must have discovered means of gathering up and storing nervous energy. Everybody has this extra reserve of force. That solved one problem. Then there was the question of a better distribution. They had to invent a new nervous system. If we ever have an opportunity of examining the Clockwork man thoroughly, we shall find out what that system is. Speaking in rough terms, we may assume that it is probably an enlargement of the compass of what we call afferent and efferent impulses. There will also be new centres, both of reflex and voluntary action. Each impulse, in this new system, has a longer range of effectiveness, a greater duration in time."

Gregg paused abruptly, as though arriving at some crisis in his thought. "It must be so. There is no other explanation to cover what we have seen. Man, as we know him, is no more or less than what his nervous system allows him to be. A creature of action, his actions are nevertheless strictly prescribed by the limitations of his neural organism. In the case of the Clockwork man we are confronted by the phenomenon of an enormous extension of nervous activity. One imagines terrific waves of energy unimpeded—or, relatively unimpeded—by the inhibitory processes that check expenditure in the case of a normal organism. Of course, there must be inhibition of some sort, but the whole system of the Clockwork man is on so grand a scale that his actions take place in a different order of time. His relapses, as he describes them, are simply the parallel of that degeneration of tissue which accompanies ordinary human fatigue. That is why his ineptitude appears ghastly to us. Again, his perceptions would be different. He would see relatively far more of the universe, and his actions would carry him further and further into the future, far beyond those laws which we have fashioned for ourselves, in accordance with our neural limitations. For, just as man is at the mercy of his nervous system, so his conception of universal laws is the natural outcome of nervous apprehension; and the universe is no more or less than what we think it is."

In his growing excitement Gregg rose and paced the floor of the room, walking away from the Doctor. He did not hear the slight snigger that broke from the latter; nor had he observed any signs of deeper incredulity in the features of his friend that might have led him to moderate his enthusiasm. He continued, in an exultant voice. "Think of what this means! We know the future! The accidental appearance of the Clockwork man may save the human race generations of striving and effort in a wrong direction. Or rather, it will save us from passing through the intermediate stages *consciously*, for everything has already happened, and the utmost we can hope is to escape the knowledge of its happening. We shall be able to take a great leap forward into the future. Once we have grasped the principle of the Clockwork man, the course of humanity is clear. It may still be several thousands of years before the final achievement, but we can at least begin."

"*NO*," thundered the Doctor, suddenly leaping to his feet. "By heavens, no. Not that!"

Gregg swung round with a gesture of annoyance. Both men were now pitched to their highest key, and every word that was spoken seemed to be charged with terrific import.

"Why not ?" said Gregg, catching his breath.

The Doctor's reply was equally breathless. "Because I, for one, refuse to accept such a responsibility. If this monstrosity is indeed the type of the future, then I reject the future. I will be no party to any attempt to reproduce him—for that, I can see, is what lurks in your mind. You would have us all clockwork men before our time! But I tell you, rather than that should happen, rather than the human race should be robbed of a few more generations of freedom, I will take steps to prevent it ever being known that the Clockwork man has paid us this visit. I will hide him. Not even you shall set eyes on him again. He shall remain an unfathomable mystery. No pagan priest ever guarded the sacred mysteries of life from an unthinking populace as I shall this enigma sprung from the womb of time! Nobody shall know. He shall remain in my keeping, a memorial to the final fall of man!"

"But why do you persist in adopting this attitude," demanded Gregg, in tones of frank disgust, "it is so frightfully reactionary."

The doctor pulled at his moustache. "I have no use for such phrases," he muttered, angrily, and began striding up and down the narrow floor space. Gregg leaned against the wall, his expression still critical.

"I won't have him," the Doctor's voice broke out again, and there was a kind of sob in it, "I won't have the Clockwork man at any price. Every nerve in my body cries out against him. He is the scandal of the ages. He must be hushed up, hidden—forgotten."

"That is already impossible. His exploits are the talk of the village."

"Let them talk," cried the Doctor, beating his head with his closed fist. "In heaven's name, let them talk the thing into a nine days wonder. Let them think he's the devil—anything rather than that they should know the truth. There may be a hundred explanations of this mystery, and yours may be the right one; I only know that I repudiate it. I cannot escape from the evidence of my own eyes; but there is something in me that denies the Clockwork man. He sticks in my gorge. Call me what you will; I am not to be shaken with phrases. The whole of man's past shrieks out against this monstrous incubus of the future. Do not ask me to offer my own explanation of the phenomenon. I have none. In vain I have stretched my brain to its bursting point in order to solve this problem. You, apparently, are ready to accept the Clockwork man as a foregone conclusion. Time alone will reveal which of us is nearer the truth."

Gregg smiled. "After all," he remarked, allowing a suitable pause to follow the Doctor's impassioned words, "it will not be for you or me to decide the matter. Our humble part will be to produce the object of the problem. Wiser men than ourselves will have to interpret its significance."

This statement might have ended the argument for the time being, had not an accident occurred that altered the whole complexion of the affair. Gregg had the wisdom to see that his friend was literally beside himself with fright and repugnance; he would have been quite content to await another opportunity for the discussion to be renewed. But at that moment the Doctor gave a cry of surprise, and stooping down picked up an object from the floor. The next moment both men were standing side by side, examining with feverish interest a further clue to the mystery.

The object that the Doctor picked up from the floor was an oblong-shaped piece of metal, almost as thin as paper, and slightly bluish in colour. Upon its surface, printed in red embossed letters, was the following matter:—

THE CLOCKWORK MAN.
DIRECTIONS FOR USE.

1. Remove hat and wig and disclose Clock.
2. Open lid of Clock by means of catch.
3. Place Clockwork man in recumbent position, face downwards.
4. Press stops A and B well home, and wind up by turning red hand. *N.B.—Great care should be taken not to over-wind.*
5. The Clockwork man should now sit up and take a little nourishment. This should be supplied at once in the form of two green tabloids (solids) and one blue

capsule (liquids). Stop C should now be pressed, and the pressure maintained until a red light appears within the bulb X.1. This registers that digestion has taken place.

On no account must any adjustment be made before the red light has appeared. Any attempt to cause function on an empty stomach will result in failure.

The Clockwork man is now ready for adjustment. The chart should be studied with care, and a choice made from one of the types indicated. Having made a selection, proceed to arrange indicators in accordance with detailed instructions, taking the utmost care to follow the directions with absolute accuracy, as the slightest error may lead to serious confusion. A good plan is to hold the chart in the left hand, and manipulate the regulators with the right, checking each adjustment as it is made.

Now wind black central hand fourteen and a half times, press centre knob until bell rings, close lid, replace wig and hat, and Clockwork man is ready for action.

The expression on Gregg's face, as he read these amazing instructions, changed slowly from avid curiosity to puzzled alarm. He was frankly embarrassed by this sudden turn of events, and for a few moments he could make nothing at all of the matter. Yet the wording was intelligible enough, and its application to the Clockwork man only too obvious. The little piece of thin metal must have slipped from his pocket during the Doctor's examination, and its discovery was undoubtedly of supreme importance.

But what could it mean? Gregg rather prided himself upon the resiliency of his mind, but not all the elasticity of which he was capable could enable him to overcome a sudden sense of uneasiness. Was the Clockwork man, after all, no more than a very elaborate and highly complex puppet?

But how could that be, since he breathed and spoke and gave every sign of the possession of an individual consciousness? Considered in this new light he was even more difficult to explain.

But when Gregg looked up, rather sheepishly, wary of meeting the Doctor's eye, he beheld a sight that sent an uncomfortable thrill down his spine. For the latter lay at full length upon the couch, his chest and stomach rising and falling in the convulsions of that excessive laughter that at first sight raises a doubt of danger in the mind of the beholder—for men have died of mirth. Gregg stared at his prostrate friend, and his own countenance was transfixed with alarm. Many minutes elapsed before any kind of definite sound brought a relief to the strain; for the Doctor's laugh was primæval; it racked his vitals, shook him from head to foot, began and stopped, proceeded in a series of explosions, not unlike those of the Clockwork man himself, until at last it reached the throat and found expression.

"Ha! ha! ha!" broke at last upon the silence of the night (and Mrs. Masters in her top attic heard the noise and thought of the devil climbing over the roofs). "Ha! ha! ha! ha!"

Gregg pulled himself together and crossed to the couch. He undid the Doctor's collar, and forced him to sit up. He thumped his back violently, at first remonstrated and then fell to the use of soothing phrases. For there was still an element of hysteria in the Doctor's manner; only now it was a symptom of release from unendurable strain. It was the hilarity of a man who has just saved his reason.

CHAPTER 10
Last Appearance of the Clockwork Man

I

IT MUST REMAIN forever a question for curious speculation as to what action might have been taken by Doctor Allingham and Gregg in conjunction, had they been able to pursue their investigation of the Clockwork man upon a thorough-going scale; for while their discussions were taking place the subject of them escaped from his confinement in the coal cellar.

Indeed, it was hardly to be expected that he would remain there for very long. As Gregg pointed out, such very delicate mechanism needed constant attention, and the unexpected was always likely to occur. There must have been some deeply-rooted automatism that gradually released the Clockwork man from his sleep; and having awakened, the grimy walls of the cellar no doubt struck him as distasteful. It was not to be expected that the Doctor, in his hurry and panic, should have succeeded in mastering the intricacies of the clock. He had merely brought about a temporary quiescence which had gradually worked off. It had to be borne in mind, also, that although the Clockwork man was dependent upon adjustment in order that he should be made to work in a right fashion, it was only too plain that he could act independently and quite wrongly.

The truth is that Doctor Allingham had not been able to summon the courage to make a further examination of the Clockwork man; and he had permitted himself to assume that there would be no immediate developments. So far as was possible he had allowed himself that very necessary relaxation, and he had insisted upon Gregg sharing it with him. The Clockwork man was not quite what either of them had, alternatively, hoped or feared. From Allingham's point of view, in particular, he was not that bogey of the inhuman fear which his original conduct had suggested. True, he was still an unthinkable monstrosity, an awful revelation; but since the discovery of the printed instructions it had been possible to regard him with a little more equanimity. The Clockwork man was a figment of the future, but he was not the whole future.

And now that he had disappeared there was a strong chance that he would never return, and that his personality and all that was connected with him would dissolve from memory of man or crystallise into a legend. That seemed a legitimate consummation of the affair, and it was the one that Doctor Allingham finally accepted. This visitation, like other alleged miracles in the past, had a meaning; and it was the meaning that mattered more than the actual miracle. To discover the significance of the Clockwork man seemed to Doctor Allingham a task worthy of the highest powers of man.

The Doctor's conclusion may be taken as a fair expression of his character. Naturally, the effect of such a preposterous revelation upon a sluggish and doubting mind would be to arouse it to a kind of furious defence of all that man has been in the past, and a scarcely less spirited rejection of that grotesque possibility of the future which the Clockwork man presented to the ordinary observer. Gregg, on the other hand, may be excused, on the score of his extreme youthfulness, for the impetuosity of his actions. His attempt to persuade the editor of the *Wide World Magazine* that his version of the affair, put in the shape of a magazine story, was actually founded on fact, ended in grotesque failure. His narrative power was not doubted; but he was advised to work the story up and introduce a little humour before offering it as a contribution to some magazine that did not vouch for the truth of its tall stories. As this was beneath Gregg's dignity, and he could find no one else to take him seriously, he shut up like an oyster, and just in time to forestall a suspicious attitude on the part of his friends. It was only years later, and after many experiences in this world of hard fact and difficult endeavour, that he began to share the Doctor's view, and to cherish the memory of the Clockwork man as a legend rich in significance.

One evening Arthur Withers and Rose Lomas sat together on their favourite stile talking in low whispers. The summer dusk lagged, and the air about them was so still that between their softly spoken words they could hear the talk of innumerable insects in the grass at their feet. There had been few interruptions. So familiar had their figures become in that position, that it had grown to be almost a tradition among the people who passed that way during the evening to cross the stile without disturbing the lovers. There are ways, too, of sitting upon a stile without incommoding the casual pedestrian.

This evening there had been one or two labourers with red, wrinkled faces, too hungry and tired to make much comment. Then Mrs. Flack had come hurrying along with her black bag (they had to get off for her as she was not so young as she had been), and soon afterwards the Curate, who beamed affably, and enquired when it was to be. He was so looking forward to uniting them.

But it was not to be yet. That was the burden of their subdued murmurings. It couldn't be done on Arthur's present income, and he was still less certain than ever that it could be regarded as cumulative or even permanent. Rose understood. To her country-bred mind it was marvellous that Arthur should succeed in adding up so many figures during the course of a day, even though the result did not always meet with the approval of the bank authorities. They would have to wait.

"It's such a responsibility," said Arthur, presently. "If we were to get married, I mean. I might come home with the sack any day."

"I shouldn't mind," protested Rose, "but I couldn't bear you to feel like that about it. We shall have to wait."

"I wonder why I'm not clever," Arthur remarked, after a long pause. Rose clutched him indignantly towards her.

"Oh, you are. The things you say. The things you think! I never knew."

And although he shook his head vigorously, Arthur inwardly contemplated that region in his mind wherein existed all the matters that comprised a knowledge quite irrelevant to the practical affairs of life but very useful for the purpose of living.

"I *do* have ideas," he admitted, thoughtfully. "I suppose I'm really what you might call an intellectual sort of chap."

"Dreadfully," said Rose, without a trace of disrespect. "The books you read!"

"Of course, I'm only a sort of amateur," Arthur continued, modestly. "But I do like books, and I can generally get at what a chap's driving at—in a way."

He stared hard at a grasshopper, who seemed to be considering the possibility of an enormous leap, for his great hind legs were taut and his long feelers caressed the air. "Sometimes I think the chaps who write books must be a bit like me—in a way. They seem to like the same things as I do. There's a lot about beauty in most books, and I like beauty, don't you?"

"Yes," breathed Rose, wondering what exactly he meant.

The grasshopper hopped and landed with a quite distinct thud, almost at their feet. They both looked at it without thinking about it at all. But its advent produced a pause.

"In the books I've read," Arthur resumed, "there's generally a chap whom you might regard as being not much good at anything and yet pretty decent."

"Heroes," suggested Rose, whose knowledge of literature was not very wide.

"Sometimes. Chaps people don't understand. That's because they like beauty more than anything else, and not many people really care about beauty. They only think of it when they see a sunset or look at pictures. If you can forget beauty, then you're alright. Nobody thinks you're strange. You don't have any difficulties."

The slight stirring of Rose's body, and a sigh so low that Arthur scarcely heard it, seemed to suggest that matters were becoming rather too deep for comprehension. The grasshopper sprung again, and this time landed upon the stile, where he remained for a long while, as though wondering what perversion of the common sense natural to grasshoppers could have prompted him to choose so barren a landing place. During the long pause

Rose did not see the look of strained perplexity upon Arthur's face.

"But they always get married," he said, suddenly. "The chaps in books, I mean. They always get married in the end."

"Oh, Arthur!" Her hand went up to pull down his, for the moment, unwilling head. "Oh, Arthur, we will get married some day."

"You're so pretty," he whispered. "You're so very beautiful."

"Oh, am I? Do you think so? I'm so glad—I'm so sorry."

Her tears gushed forth, inexplicably, even to Arthur, who thought he understood so much that was difficult to understand. He had let loose his feeling without any real knowledge of its depth, or that which it aroused in Rose.

"I can't bear you not to have me," she sobbed. "It's cruel. It ought to be arranged. People ought to understand."

Arthur was startled back to common sense. "They don't," he whispered, as they held one another in trembling arms. "If they did they would be like us."

And then he remembered a possible sequel to the search for beauty.

"Besides," he added, in a formal whisper, "there's the children."

III

Along the path that led from Bapchurch to Great Wymering there walked two persons, slowly, and with an air of having talked themselves into embarrassed silence. Their steps were gradually bringing them to the stile upon which Arthur and Rose sat.

"That last remark of yours cut me to the quick," said the Doctor, at last.

"I meant it to," said Lilian, firmly. "I want you to be cut to the quick. It's our only chance."

"Of what?" enquired the Doctor, conscious of masculine stupidity.

"Of loving somehow. Oh, don't you understand? I want to care for you, but you're making it impossible. You *will* jest about the things sacred to me. Your flippant tongue destroys everything. It's as I said just now. I like my friends to be humorous; but my lover must be serious."

"But I can't help it," pleaded the Doctor. "Take away my humour and I'm frightened at what's left of myself. There's nothing but an appalling chaos."

"Because you are afraid of life," said Lilian. "Men have laughed their way through the ages; women have wept and lived. I can't share your world of assumptions and rule of thumb laws. To me love is a chaos, a dear confusion—a divine muddle. It's creation itself, an indefinite proceeding beginning with God."

The Doctor harked back in his mind to the beginning of their talk. "But you objected to my house," he mused, "that was how the discussion arose. And now we've got somewhere up in the stars."

Lilian glanced up at them. "If only we could keep there! By their habitations are men known. A house ought to be a sort of resting place. No more. Once you elaborate it, it becomes a prison, with hard labour attached."

"But where does all this lead?" pondered the Doctor, half falling in with her mood. "Why not make some things permanent and as good as they can be?"

"Because they are only part of ourselves, only so many additions to the human organism, extra bits of brain. We're slowly discovering that. Humanity daren't be permanent, except in its fundamentals, and all the fundamentals have to do with living and being. Just think what would happen if the blood in your veins became permanent?"

"Death," said the Doctor, "speaking from knowledge rather than from symbolical conviction."

"Well, then," resumed Lilian, triumphantly, "isn't all this possession of things, all this wanting to have and keep, a sort of death, beginning from the extremities? Wouldn't it be awful if the human body didn't change, if we got fixed in some way, didn't grow old or lose our hair, or have influenza?"

The Doctor paused in his walk. How strange that Lilian should say that! It almost seemed as though she must have heard about the Clockwork man!

And then they both stopped, and at the same moment saw Rose and Arthur seated on the stile.

"Let's go back," whispered Lilian, and they turned and retraced their steps. The sight of the lovers sealed their lips. Doctor Allingham struggled for a few moments with a strange sense of bigness wanting to escape. Almost it was a physical sensation; as though the nervous energy in his brain had begun to flow independently of the controls that usually guided it through the channels graven by knowledge and experience. It was Lilian who spoke next, and there was a note of pain in her voice.

"Oh, why are we troubled like this? Why can't we be like *them*? We shan't ever get any nearer happiness this way. We shan't ever be better than those two. We've simply got a few more thoughts, a little more knowledge—and it may be quite the wrong kind of knowledge."

"Then why—" began the Doctor, as though this begged the whole question.

"Oh, wait," said Lilian, "I had to have it out with you. I had to talk of these things, as though talking's any good! I couldn't let you just take me for granted. Don't you see? I suppose all this talk between us is nothing but an extension of the age-long process of mating. I'm just like the primitive woman running away from her man."

The Doctor paused in his walk and took hold of her elbows. "Does that mean that you've been playing with me all this time?"

"Coquette," smiled Lilian, "only it's not been conscious until this moment. Somehow those two reminded me. There's always this dread of capture with us women, and nowadays it's more complicated and extended. Yes, thought does give us longer life. Everything has a larger prelude. I've been afraid of your big house, which will be such a nuisance to look after. I've been afraid of a too brief honeymoon, and then of you becoming a cheerful companion at meals and a regular winder up of clocks." She laughed hysterically. "And then you might do wood-carving in the winter evenings."

"Not on your life," roared the Doctor. "At the worst I shall bore you with my many-times-told jests."

"And at the best I shall learn to put up with them," said Lilian. "That's where my sense of humour will come in."

The Doctor suddenly took her in his arms. "But you care?" he whispered. "You consent to make me young again?"

She stirred curiously in his arms, her mind newly alert.

"Oh, I never thought of that. How stupid we clever people are! I never thought that being a lover would make you young."

"Ignoramus," laughed the Doctor. "A woman's first child is always her husband."

"You and your epigrams!"

"You and your thoughts!"

She joined in his mirth. A little later it was before she had the last word.

"Creation," she whispered, "I don't believe it's happened yet. That seven days and seven nights is still going on. Man has yet to be created, and woman must help to create him."

IV

"I must be getting back," said the Clockwork man to himself, as he trundled slowly over the hump of the meadow and approached the stile. "I shall only make a muddle of things here."

There was still a touch of complaint in his voice, as though he felt sorry now to leave a world so full of pitfalls and curious adventures. Something brisker about his appearance seemed to suggest that an improvement had taken place in his working arrangements. You might have thought him rather an odd figure, stiff-necked, and jerky in his gait; but there were no lapses into his early bad manner.

"I have a feeling," he continued, placing a finger to his nose, "that if I put on my top gear now I should be off like a shot."

But he did not hurry. He twisted his head gradually round as though to embrace as much as possible in his last survey of a shapely, if limited world.

"Such a jolly little place," he mused. "You could have such fun—and be yourself. I wonder why it reminds me so of something—before the days of the clock, before we *knew*."

He sighed, and suddenly stopped in order to contemplate the two figures seated together on the stile. Rose was asleep in Arthur's arms.

"Don't bother," said the Clockwork man, as Arthur stirred slightly, "I'm not going that way. I shall go back the way I came."

"Oh," said Arthur, smitten with embarrassment, "then I shan't see you again?"

"Not for a few thousand years," replied the Clockwork man, with a slight twisting of his lip. "Perhaps never."

"Are you better now?" Arthur enquired.

"I'm working alright, if that's what you mean," said the other, averting his eyes. Then he looked very hard at Rose, and the expression on his features altered to mild astonishment.

"Why are you holding that other person like that?" he asked.

"She's my sweetheart," Arthur replied.

"You must explain that to me. I've forgotten the formula."

Arthur considered. "I'm afraid it can't be explained," he murmured, "it just is."

The Clockwork man winked one eye slowly, and at the same time there begun a faint spinning noise, very remote and detached. As Arthur looked at him he noticed another singularity. Down the smooth surface of the Clockwork man's face there rolled two enormous tears. They descended each cheek simultaneously, keeping exact pace.

"I remember now," the mechanical voice resumed, with something like a throb in it, "all that old business—before we became *fixed*, you know. But they had to leave it out. It would have made the clock too complicated. Besides, it wasn't necessary, you see. The clock kept you going for ever. The splitting up process went out of fashion, the splitting up of yourself into little bits that grew up like you—offspring, they used to call them."

Arthur dimly comprehended this. "No children," he hazarded.

The Clockwork man shook his head slowly from side to side. "No children. No love—nothing but going on for ever, spinning in infinite space and knowledge."

He looked directly at Arthur. "And dreaming," he added. "We dream, you know."

"Yes?" Arthur murmured, interested.

"The dream states," explained the Clockwork man, "are the highest point in clock evolution. They are very expensive, because it is a costly process to manufacture a dream. It's all rolled up in a spool, you see, and then you fit it into the clock and unroll it. The dreams are like life, only of course they aren't real. And then there are the records, you know, the music records. They fit into the clock as well."

"But do you all have clocks?" Arthur ventured. "Are you born with them?"

"We're not born," said the Clockwork man, looking vaguely annoyed, "we just are. We've remained the same since the first days of the clock." He ruminated, his forehead corrugated into regular lines. "Of course, there are the others, the *makers*, you know."

"The makers?" echoed Arthur.

"Yes, you wouldn't know about them, although you're not unlike a maker yourself. Only you wear clothes like us, and the makers don't wear clothes. That was what puzzled me about you. The look in your eyes reminded me of a maker. They came after the last wars. It's all written in history. There was a great deal of fighting and killing and blowing up and poisoning, and then the makers came and they didn't fight. It was they who invented the clock for us, and after that every man had to have a clock fitted into him, and then he didn't have to fight any more, because he could move about in a multiform world where there was plenty of room for everybody."

"But didn't the other people object?" said Arthur.

"Object to what?"

"To having the clock fitted into them."

"Would you object," said the Clockwork man, "to having all your difficulties solved for you?"

"I suppose not," Arthur admitted, humbly.

"That was what the makers did for man," resumed the other. "Life had become impossible, and it was the only practical way out of the difficulty. You see, the makers were very clever, and very mild and gentle. They were quite different to ordinary human beings. To begin with, they were *real*."

"But aren't you real?" Arthur could not refrain from asking.

"Of course not," rapped out the Clockwork man, "I'm only an invention."

"But you look real," objected Arthur.

The Clockwork man emitted a faint, cacophonous cackle.

"We feel real when the dream states unroll within us, or the music records. But the makers *are* real, and they live in the real world. No clockwork man is allowed to get back into the real world. The clock prevents us from doing that. It was because we were such a nuisance and got in the way of the makers that they invented the clock."

"But what is the real world like?" questioned Arthur.

"How can I know?" said the Clockwork man, flapping his ears in despair. "I'm *fixed*. I can't be anything beyond what the clock permits me to be. Only, since I've been in your world, I've had a suspicion. It's such a jolly little place. And you have women."

Arthur caught his breath. "No women?"

"No. You see, the makers kept all the women because they were more real, and they didn't want the fighting to go on, or the world that the men wanted. So the makers took the women away from us and shut us up in the clocks and gave us the world we wanted. But they left us no loophole of escape into the real world, and we can neither laugh nor cry properly."

"But you try," suggested Arthur.

"It's only breakdown," said the Clockwork man, sadly. "With us laughing or crying are symptoms of breakdown. When we laugh or cry that means that we have to go and get oiled or adjusted. Something has got out of gear. Because in our life there's no necessity for these things."

His voice trailed away and ended in a soft, tinkling sound, like sheep bells heard in the distance. During the long pause that followed Arthur had time to recall that sense of pity for this grotesque being which had accompanied his first impression of him; but now his feeling swelled into an infinite compassion, and with it there came to him a fierce questioning fever.

"But must you always be like this?" he began, with a suppressed crying note in his voice. "Is there no hope for you?"

"None," said the Clockwork man, and the word was boomed out on a hollow, brassy note. "We are made, you see. For us creation is finished.

We can only improve ourselves very slowly, but we shall never quite escape the body of this death. We've only ourselves to blame. The makers gave us our chance. They are beings of infinite patience and forbearance. But they saw that we were determined to go on as we were, and so they devised this means of giving us our wish. You see, Life was a Vale of Tears, and men grew tired of the long journey. The makers said that if we persevered we should come to the end and know joys earth has not seen. But we could not wait, and we lost faith. It seemed to us that if we could do away with death and disease, with change and decay, then all our troubles would be over. So they did that for us, and we've stopped the same as we were, except that time and space no longer hinder us."

He broke off and struggled with some queer kind of mechanical emotion. "And now they play games with us. They wind us up and make us do all sorts of things, just for fun. They try all sorts of experiments with us, and we can't help ourselves because we're in their power; and if they like they can stop the clock, and then we aren't anything at all."

"But that's not very kind of them," suggested Arthur.

"Oh, they don't hurt us. We don't feel any pain or annoyance, only a dim sort of revolt, and even that can be adjusted. You see, the makers can ring the changes endlessly with us, and there isn't any kind of being, from a great philosopher to a character out of a book, that we can't be turned into by twisting a hand. It's all very wonderful, you know."

He lifted his arms up and dropped them again sharply.

"You wouldn't believe some of the things we can do. The clock is a most wonderful invention! And the economy. Some of the hands, you see, can be used for quite different purposes. Twist them so many times and you have a politician; twist a little more and you have a financier. Press one stop slightly and we talk about the divinity of man; press harder and there will issue from us nothing but blasphemy. Tighten a screw and we are altruists; loosen it and we are beasts. You see, generations ago it was known exactly the best and worst that man could be; and the makers like to amuse themselves by going over it again. There isn't any best or worst with them."

"But you," entreated Arthur, "what is your life like?"

Again the tears flowed down the Clockwork man's cheeks, this time in a sequence of regular streams.

"We have only one hope, and even that is an illusion. Sometimes we think the makers will take us seriously in the end, and so perfect the mechanism that we shall be like them. But how can they? How can they—unless—unless—"

"Unless what?" eagerly enquired Arthur, fearful of a final collapse.

"Unless we die," said the Clockwork man, clicking slightly, "unless we consent to be broken up and put into the earth, and wait while we slowly turn into little worms, and then into big worms; and then into clumsy, crawling creatures, and finally come back again to the Vale of Tears." He swayed slightly, with a finger lodged against his nose. "But it will take such a frightful time, you know. That's why we chose to have the clock. We were impatient. We were tired of waiting. The makers said we must have patience; and we could not get patience. They said that creation really took place in the twinkling of an eye, and we must have patience."

"Patience!" echoed Arthur. "Yes, I think they were right. We must have patience. We have to wait."

For a few moments the Clockwork man struggled along with a succession of staccato sentences and irrelevant words, and finally seemed to realise that the game was up. "I can't go on like this," he concluded, in a shrill undertone. "I ought not to have tried to talk like this. It upsets the mechanism. I wasn't meant for this sort of thing. I must go now."

He began to grow dim. Arthur, instinctively polite, stretched out a hand, keeping his left arm round Rose. The Clockwork man veered slightly forward. He seemed to realise Arthur's intention and offered a vibrating hand. But they missed each other by several days.

"Oh, don't you see?" the faint voice asseverated.

"But what are we to do?" said Arthur, raising his voice. "Tell us what we must do to avoid following you?"

"I don't know." The thin voice sounded like someone shouting in the distance. "How should I know? It's all so difficult. But don't make it more difficult than you can help. Keep smiling—laughter—such a jolly little world."

He was fading rapidly.

"Come back," shouted Arthur, scarcely knowing why he was so in earnest. "You must come back and tell us."

"Wallabaloo," echoed through the months. "Wum—wum—"

"What's that?" Rose exclaimed, suddenly awakened.

"Hark," said Arthur, clutching her tightly. "Be quiet—I want to listen for something."

"Nine and ninepence—" he heard at last, very thin and distinct. And then there was stillness.

THE END